HER REBELLION

THE RITE TRILOGY BOOK 2

A. ZAVARELLI

NATASHA KNIGHT

Copyright © 2022 by A. Zavarelli & Natasha Knight
All rights reserved.
No part of this book may be reproduced in any form or by any electronic or mechanical means, including information storage and retrieval systems, without written permission from the author, except for the use of brief quotations in a book review.

This is a work of fiction. Names, characters, places and incidents are either the product of the author's imagination or are used fictitiously, and any resemblance to actual persons, living or dead, business establishments, events, or locales is purely coincidental.

ABOUT THIS BOOK

Her Rebellion is Book 2 of *The Rite Trilogy* and must be read in order.

If you haven't yet read *His Rule*, you should do that first. It is available in all stores now.

The Rite Trilogy is set in the world of The Society. It is the story of Mercedes De La Rosa and Judge Montgomery and the trilogy can be read as a standalone series.

If you're new to The Society and would like to read the first series of books in the world, you can start with Requiem of the Soul. You can find more details and store links by clicking here.

1

JUDGE

I check my watch when the knock comes on my study door. Miriam is prompt, as I expect. "Enter."

"You wanted to see me, sir?" she asks, eyebrows raised in confusion.

"I did. Come in and close the door."

"It's late, sir. I was—"

"This won't take long."

She nods, closes the door, and comes to stand before the desk. I've set one chair there. A low wooden one. Uncomfortable. Small.

"Sit, Miriam."

She sits, arranges her usual black dress over her knees, and finally meets my gaze.

I set the paperweight on the center of the desk and watch her stunned reaction. The only sound is a tiny intake of breath as color leaches from her face.

"She didn't lie, did she?" I ask, somehow calm even though what I want to do is the opposite of that. It's violence. Pure and simple.

"I don't know what you mean, sir." She folds her legs one way, then the other. Then she stands. "I'm tired. My shift is over. Perhaps we can—"

"Fucking. Sit."

She lowers herself, her knees trembling.

"You've been feeding my mother information."

"Your mother? No, sir. I work for you."

"Ah, but you and she, well, with your brother being Theron's father, I imagine you're all very close." That's what I discovered after a little bit of digging. It didn't even take that much. She used her ex-husband's name on her initial application years ago. Somehow it slipped past my grandfather although maybe he didn't care who my mother took for a housekeeper. She lived in the cottage by then. It's not like he ever had to see either of them.

"It's not like that," she croaks out.

"You kicked her when she was down. Literally and figuratively."

She swallows hard.

"You could have killed her."

"Sir…"

"And I believed you. The black eyes were convincing. How did you do it?"

Nothing.

"It doesn't matter. What matters is what I did," I say more to myself than her.

"I'll gather my things." She starts to rise again.

"Did you hear me dismiss you?"

She drops back into her seat.

"And no, you won't gather your things. Because if you do, you'll be going directly to a prison cell."

"Sir, it wasn't my intention. I never would have hurt her."

"Oh, I think you would have, but let's go ahead and discuss that, shall we? Whose plan was it?"

She hesitates. "No, I really... I mean... She was so cruel to me. So belittling. You bringing her here like that brought her down a notch."

"And you wanted to bring her down a few more."

"She's spoiled. You said it yourself."

"How do you know what I said?"

She looks around the room.

"Walls seem to be remarkably thin in this house."

She nods like an idiot.

"Did you tell her I gave her my permission to ride with Theron that afternoon?"

She clears her throat.

"Why?" I ask.

She shakes her head, eyes wet although I'm pretty sure any tears she sheds are to save her own skin and not for any remorse she may feel.

"Answer me."

"We thought maybe Theron…"

"You thought to put Mercedes in his path. You and my mother."

She lowers her gaze to the floor.

"What else does my mother know?"

She stares at me with her stupid eyes. She's not the brains behind this operation.

"How you answer me will decide what I do with you, and prison is a very real possibility."

"I… The courtesan."

Fuck.

I keep my face neutral and impassive as if it means nothing at all. Because it means everything. Because if my mother knows what Mercedes did, she can cause real trouble for her. And she will if it will serve her.

I need to think. To get ahead of this. I have fucked this up so royally.

"Here's what's going to happen, Miriam." She looks up at me and wipes her eyes and her nose. Snivels like a pig. "You are going to pretend this conversation never happened."

She's surprised at this. Nods enthusiastically. "Of course, sir. Of course! Thank you!"

"Don't be so eager. If my mother or Theron get wind of this, if they find out that I know, I will haul you to a jail cell so fast you won't know what hit you. Am I clear?"

"But... sir..."

I pick up the paperweight and toss it from one hand to the other as her face turns a shade of gray I didn't know was possible for a living, breathing human being.

"And according to your file," I say, opening the single folder on my desk. "It won't be your first time. You were in prison before. Petty crimes but enough of them. I don't imagine you liked it much. Inmates are brutal, aren't they?" I give that a long minute to sink in. "None of the comings and goings of this house will be discussed with my mother or brother. Understood?"

"Yes, sir."

I get to my feet, walk around the desk, and loom over her. "And if Mercedes so much as feels you've looked at her the wrong way, there will be hell to pay. Am I very fucking clear on that point, Miriam?"

A knock on the door interrupts our conversation. I barely have a moment to be pissed because whoever it is doesn't wait for me to give the order to enter but keeps knocking and pushes the door open at the same time.

It's Lois, which surprises me, but it's the look on her face that has my heart drop to my stomach.

"Get out, Miriam." I don't wait for her to move but pick her up by her arm and give her a good shove toward the door. Lois gives her just enough space to clear the room, and I hear her running down the hall.

But I don't care about Miriam. Because Lois is crying, shaking, too upset to speak.

I take her arms, squeeze.

"What is it? What the hell has happened?"

"She's gone. She's just..."

"What?"

"Mercedes. She was feeling sick so I opened the window to give her some fresh air and—"

"The window?" She's up on the second floor.

Lois nods. "She used sheets."

I run past her up to Mercedes's room and crash through the door to find it and the bathroom empty. The window is open, and it wouldn't be wide enough for me to squeeze out, but Mercedes is smaller than me and much more flexible. But that's not the worst of it. There, outside, Paolo is gathering up the sheets that she'd tied together, that had ripped from whatever she'd secured them to. The dogs are sniffing and barking, and I hurry back out of her room and down the stairs through the kitchen and out the door.

A memory of something I'd seen at her house crops up in my head. A magazine. Yoga. Aerial yoga.

But fuck. To tie sheets together and use them in an attempt to escape? And go where? The gate is locked. She can't get off the property, and if she could, then what? She has no money. No transportation.

Although she has friends. Friends outside of IVI.

And she has one on property. An accomplice more likely.

Theron.

"Did she fall?" I ask, my heart pounding against my chest when I reach Paolo.

He holds out the ripped sheet.

"Fuck!" Did my brother come get her? Did he somehow plan her escape? Did Miriam facilitate it? For all I know, he could be running off to elope with her. But she wouldn't do that to me. She wouldn't.

At least she survived the fall. There's no blood. Nothing like that.

I dig my phone out of my pocket and dial my brother. After a few rings, it goes to voicemail, and I hear his arrogant voice commanding me to leave a message.

"Where the fuck is she? Pick up the goddamn phone, you little prick!" I disconnect, then hurry to the stable to get my horse. The grounds are acres large, and the South Cottage is at the farthest end of the property with its own entrance and exit. I need to take the detour to the stables because it will be faster to get there by horse than on foot.

As I mount, I call Theron again, and it again goes to voicemail after a few rings.

"If you touch her, I will fucking kill you." I disconnect and ride at the speed of light to his cottage, keeping low to Kentucky Lightning's back as we take the shortest route through the woods.

I hear the dogs somewhere nearby. They must have picked up her scent. But I'm surprised when the sound of their barking grows farther away. When Theron's cottage comes into view, it's dark. No lights are on. No smoke from the fireplace. His car is in the driveway, but the house is empty. I know it. He's not here.

And my alarm grows. Because this is more wrong than my brother stealing her away just to fuck with me. I feel the dread in my gut.

On the wind, I hear the whining of the dogs. I squeeze my thighs around Kentucky Lightning's body and turn him in the direction from where the barking grows louder.

But it's farther off than it should be, in a direction I don't expect. And as I near the outbuildings, passing the one I'd kept Ivy in, my blood runs cold.

Because there's one place I've forbidden her. Would she go there? Would he take her there?

I stop thinking as I approach the dark mouth of the entrance because I hear a terrifying scream, and my gut wrenches.

"Mercedes!" The wind carries my call away. Can she hear me in there?

Another scream is followed by a choked sob, and I hurry blindly through the darkness, stumbling over stones. When I reach the door, all I can think is I don't have the key but that doesn't matter because the lock is gone. Someone has cut it out. I push my way in, and I don't know if it's the ear-piercing scream or the sight that greets me that makes my vision darken, makes my brain rattle inside my skull.

Because there, naked and bound to the leather-topped bench I remember well, is Mercedes up on the tips of her toes because she wouldn't reach the handholds otherwise. She barely reaches them now. Her arms are stretched too far, her hair sweeping the filthy floor. But the worst of it. Fuck. The worst of it is the soft, fragile skin of her ass and thighs burns a throbbing, angry red, the skin broken in places, a drop of crimson blood sliding over the crease of one knee as she sobs like I've never heard anyone sob.

And behind her stands Theron. He's shirtless and covered in sweat, holding a cane in his hand. A whip is discarded at his feet. The look on his face, in his eyes, that's not the brother I know even in his cruelest moments. Even when he put the knife in my back.

That man was human.

This one I don't recognize.

But when he raises the cane again, I don't think. I can't over the roaring rush of blood that deafens me. Or maybe that's my own scream when I charge him. Because I'm going to fucking kill him.

2

MERCEDES

Fire singes my nerve endings and ricochets through my body as an almighty roar unleashes behind me. It sounds like a demon sent straight from hell, but I know without a shadow of a doubt it isn't. He's not quite the devil, but he's no angel either. It has to be Judge.

I try to peel my face up off the leather when I hear a grunt, followed by a commotion, but I'm too weak. I try to call out for him, needing confirmation it's going to be okay now, but my lips are too parched, and I have no voice left from screaming.

A muttered curse from his lips is the proof I need, and then all at once my body gives out. Like a thousand-pound weight has been lifted off my shoulders, I have to believe it will be okay. It will be okay because he's here. That thought fades into oblivion as the adrenaline crashes, my head swims, and I succumb to the blackness.

Something tickles the edges of my consciousness, warmth blooming beneath my skin. I feel hot. Feverish. Like I'm burning alive. Pain skitters across my flesh, dragging me back to the reality I'd hoped to forget. It wasn't a dream. It wasn't a nightmare. I was there, and now, it's too quiet. I'm scared to open my eyes. Scared to move. My heart feels like it's going to beat out of my chest, and I'm struggling to draw in a breath when a palm comes to rest on my cheek.

"Mercedes."

I jolt away from the touch, flopping onto my back, only to let out an agonized cry when I do. *The pain. Oh, God, the pain.*

My chest caves in, and before I can understand what's happening, I'm wracked with sobs. Deep, ugly, horrifying sobs.

"Please," the choked voice beside me whispers. "Open your eyes. Look at me."

That voice... the sound of my tormentor and my savior has the strangest effect. It wounds me, yet it brings me a small sort of comfort. Because I know for certain, he has reclaimed me. I have traded one monster for another, and I have to believe this is the lesser evil.

"Please," Judge begs. "Look at me."

In the span of a few shuddering heartbeats, I

manage to open my eyes. Not for him. Never again for him. But when I meet his gaze, the anguish on his face steals my breath away.

"Let me help you," he says softly. Softer than I've ever heard him speak. "I need to roll you back onto your side, so it doesn't hurt. But that means I need to touch you. Will you let me?"

Another wave of sobbing commences, and it can't be helped. I don't have control of my emotions right now. I don't have control of my own mind.

"Fucking Christ." Judge reaches out to touch me again, and again, I flinch away, cutting him deep. I can see it in his eyes. He looks so helpless, and he has never been a helpless man.

I have never been a helpless woman either. But right now, I am. I'm so completely fractured beyond repair I don't know if I'll ever recover from this.

"Perhaps I should try," Lois offers in a gentle tone as she steps forward.

For a moment, Judge looks so utterly broken by the idea he shakes his head. But my eyes move to Lois, and I reach my fingers toward her in a silent plea. She's the only person who hasn't hurt me here. My only ally in this house.

"Okay," Judge concedes with a stiff tone. "Please, just get her onto her side."

Lois sits down beside me, careful and deliberate as she reaches out to touch my arm. "I'm going to help you turn back this way," she says gently. "Is it okay if I touch your shoulder?"

I nod at her with a jerk of my chin, and she positions her hand beneath my shoulder and slowly rolls me back onto my side, legs curled into my body. My ass stings. My thighs too. But something sticky coats my skin, and I know they must have salved the wounds.

"Is that okay?" she asks.

Again, I nod, grateful for her soothing energy.

"We have some medication that will help," she tells me. "Will you take it?"

My eyes move back to Judge, and my body shakes as another wave of agony pulses through me.

"I'll be right here." He leans forward onto his elbows, his brows pinched in frustration. "I'm not going anywhere, sweetheart. Nobody will touch you. Nobody will ever hurt you like that again."

My lips part, and I release a strangled sound, working my dry throat until I can force a response from it. "Don't make promises... you can't keep."

Devastation passes over his face, but I'm too far gone to care. When I glance up at Lois, she seems to understand what I need. A promise from someone I can actually trust.

"I'll stay," she assures me. "Please, Mercedes,

do not worry. I will watch over you. But you need to rest. You need to heal."

I nod, and she takes the pills from Judge, along with a small cup of water. She has to hold my head up so I can take them, and when I do, my eyes feel heavy within seconds. I'm exhausted, and Lois is right. The only thing I can do now is rest.

Hours blur into each other. Moments of oblivion seem to fracture under seconds of brief clarity when I open my eyes to find Lois kept her word. She hasn't left. Neither has Judge.

Images of them at my bedside swirl through my mind, getting tangled up somewhere in the brutal nightmares that seem to possess my body and mind. Screams pierce the silence, and I tremble so violently, I wonder if I'm actually dying. When they try to comfort me, it only makes it worse.

"What can we do?" I hear Judge's voice. And then someone else. The doctor, I think.

"Time." His words fade away, morphing into something else.

Hellhounds are chasing me through the dark forest, nipping at my heels. My screams seem to echo all around me, the sound reverberating through my chest and down into the ground, only to rumble beneath my feet. I dare a glance over my shoulder, gasping for breath, only to realize they aren't hounds at all. They are beasts with men's faces. All the men who have ever hurt me.

Lorenzo De La Rosa, my father. Santiago. Theron. And of course, Judge.

I try to fight them off. I try to keep them at bay with a large stick, but just like all the other times, I am no match. One by one, they pounce on me and tear at my flesh, eating me alive until there's nothing left but my frail, beating heart.

"Vivid dreams," a voice murmurs around me. "Side effect."

I strain to hear the rest, but suddenly, I'm pulled back into my father's office as if through a vortex. Back to a time when I decided it would be a good idea to show him I had a backbone. He seems larger than life in his deathly form. Looming over the desk as he leans forward, his face half eviscerated from the explosion, exposing his skull. When his arms move, he hovers closer to the ceiling, and black smoke curls around the room, suffocating the air.

Foolish little girl. His words reverberate through me, chilling me to the bone. And then, just as before, he's dragging me to the chapel to mete out my punishment all over again.

The marble is so cold against my cheek when he tosses me down. I cry because it has to be real.

But it's the sound of him pulling his belt free that truly douses me in terror.

The leather slices into my skin, and I jolt, only to be slammed back down by his boot. And then he repeats it. Over and over. The violence has no end, and my tears won't save me, even when my limbs start to fall apart, tearing at the seams.

"Please," I beg.

"Bad girls go to hell!" he roars as the floor opens up to a fiery pit, and I'm falling, falling down to the depths of the inferno to burn for all of eternity.

"Mercedes, please." Gentle fingers touch my face, and my eyelashes flutter, pulling me back from the clutches of my mind. "Wake up."

I want to, but I'm still too afraid. And then I smell him. Warm spices and leather. I tell myself it isn't safe. I can't trust anyone. But when I feel his weight dipping against the bed next to me, I wish I could.

"Wake up." His fingers move over my jaw, stroking my skin like he's memorizing it. "I know you're in there."

My eyes flicker open gradually, and the bright sunlight stings, disorienting me. How long have I been in this bed? I try to move, and Judge's warm breath blows across my lips as he stills me. He's so close, lying right beside me, face-to-face. Dark circles color the skin beneath his eyes. Exhaustion hangs heavy in his features, but there's relief there too.

"It's okay now," he murmurs. "I'm here with you."

I wish I could believe him. When I blink, more tears come, and I'm so tired of crying. But Judge wipes them away with his thumbs, his body moving closer yet. His warmth penetrates me, and I don't want to like it. I don't want to be comforted by it. But I can't bring myself to push him away. Not even when he drags his fingers over my lips like all he wants to do is kiss them, but he knows not to try.

"How long have I been here?" I croak.

"Days," he answers with a solemn tone.

I don't understand how that's possible. I don't remember sleeping for days. Or drinking. Or going to the bathroom. But I'm clean and in a fresh pair of pajamas when I glance down. And there's an IV in my hand, the tube leading to a stand next to the bed.

"Have I woken?" I ask.

"At times." Darkness flashes in his vision like he doesn't want to recall those moments. "But we've been keeping you medicated. You may not remember."

My eyes drift to his, and I find myself getting lost in them, wondering who he really is. Wondering what he hides from the world.

Theron's words are still fresh in my mind. *You don't know what he's capable of.*

"Why are you here?" I ask.

"Because." He swallows painfully. "I can't… leave you."

I want to understand the emotion behind those words, but I can't. Exhaustion is weighing me down again, pulling me under fast. Judge senses it, and he moves closer, brushing the hair away from my face before his palm settles on my waist.

"It's okay," he whispers, his words a sweet lullaby in my ear. "You can sleep now, little monster. I'll watch over you. You're safe with me now."

3

JUDGE

The door gives easily. It's why I heard her scream from outside. It wasn't fully closed, or I wouldn't have heard her at all. That's the point of the punishment room. No one to hear you. No one to rescue you.

But he took the lock out. The handle lies on the ground. It's no longer possible to close it.

The sight that greets me is both something out of the past and a thing that should never, ever have come to pass. Mercedes is here. Mercedes is in the room where my grandfather yielded to the monster inside himself. Where beast overtook man.

She's bound to the whipping bench. Her body stretched too far. Long limbs not long enough.

Her mouth opens on a scream as Theron's blow lands, but that scream is caught. Halted. She must hear me and know that I'm here. That I've come for her. And *for one fleeting but undeniable moment, I see hope in her eyes. Relief.*

Then her head drops. Her body jolts as my brother lays down one more stroke across the backs of her thighs and I swear I smell the copper of blood. But maybe that's an old smell that clings to the walls here. Like his cigars.

I charge him then. With an almighty roar and a rage unleashed, I charge him.

But he's slow to process because he turns his head to me but remains still. He doesn't run. Doesn't raise his arms to protect himself. He just watches with the strangest grin on his face. A look of what? Satisfaction? Satisfaction at what he's done? Breaking a woman half his size? Or is it satisfaction to see he's unleashed the beast inside me?

Because at this moment, I am my grandfather.

I take him down, knocking the cane from his hand. He doesn't fight. Not at first. He laughs this strange, madman's laugh.

Theron's head bounces off the floor as we crash down, his body breaking my fall.

"What the hell are you doing?" I trap him beneath my thighs and pound my fist into his jaw so violently that I wonder if I didn't break it. But there's that sound again. That laughter.

Unhinged.

Insane.

Inhuman.

He turns his eyes to me and in the dim light I see how dilated his pupils are. See the sheen of sweat on his forehead, the unnatural flush of his cheeks. He looks almost ill.

That could be exertion though. From whipping Mercedes to the point of breaking skin.

So I draw my arm back and smash my fist into his temple this time and I don't give him a chance to recover before getting up, hauling him to his feet and throwing him against the stone wall.

Air whooshes from his lungs and when he catches his breath, I hear that laughter again, a high-pitched sound. "There he is!"

My fist meets his gut, and he doubles over with a grunt. "Let's see you fight me, you fucking bastard. Or don't you dare to fight someone who is your equal in size and strength?"

He raises his head, that grin gone, his blue eyes almost black. "Oh, no, brother. I dare." He charges me, screaming, and I see too late the wooden paddle he must have grabbed off the wall at his back as he brings it down across the side of my head with a force that makes my brain rattle.

I stumble backward and he comes at me again. My vision is double, but I bend to tackle him knocking him to the ground.

"I'm going to kill you," I tell him, smashing his wrist, throwing the paddle from his grip.

"I have no doubt," he manages as I rain blows

down on his face again and again and again. Blood splatters across my cheeks, my eyes. It blurs my vision and I taste the coppery tang of it on my lip. Theron's face is slowly becoming unrecognizable but then I hear a moan. Mercedes.

I stop, turn to her. Her limp body is still flopped over the bench. But she's waking. And she can't see me like this.

"Mercedes!" I stagger to my feet. My knuckles are raw, my knees hurt, and the room spins so I have to grab the corner of a nearby table to steady myself. I look down at my brother who lies unmoving in a bloody heap. He may be dead for all I know but he groans when I trip over him, not yet steady from the hit to my head.

He's not dead. Not yet. Good. I'll do the job properly later. First, I need to tend to Mercedes. I need to get to her.

But just as I reach her, she's gone. Like every other time.

"Judge. Judge, wake up."

I grab the hand that's shaking me and leap from my seat.

Lois gasps, her eyes huge. I blink, and look at her face. Then down at how I'm holding her.

"You were having a nightmare," she says as I release her. I step away in shame.

"I'm sorry. I'm sorry if I hurt you." Fuck. I gave in to the monster inside me when I beat Theron.

Will it no longer sleep? Is it hungry for more now that it's had a taste?

"It's alright. You didn't hurt me."

She tries to give me a reassuring smile, fails, and turns her worried gaze to Mercedes.

"Has it begun?" she asks. She doesn't have to say what. The nightmares. They're a nightly occurrence. She's asking if they've begun today.

"Not yet."

She glances at the nearly untouched tray on the table. She brought my dinner in a few hours ago. Although I'm not hungry I forced down a little food.

"You need to eat a full meal and get some rest. You can't keep going like this. I can spend the night with her."

"I'm fine."

She watches me and I know what she's thinking. Is it safe for me to be around Mercedes? What if I grab her like I did Lois? I've been reliving that night just like Mercedes is every time I close my eyes and given the exhaustion, I am not myself.

"I won't hurt her," I tell Lois in a voice I don't recognize.

"I know you won't," she says after too long.

Jesus. God. Is it better if I'm away from her?

Mercedes moans then. Says my name. It's the first time she's called for me since she's been in here.

Lois and I both look at her and something blooms in my chest at the sound. Because she's turning her face into the pillow where I usually lie beside her. Is she searching for me?

"You won't hurt her," Lois reassures me, a hand on my arm. "Go to her. She needs you."

Mercedes sleeps a little better when I'm beside her. It's some comfort to me, that knowledge. When the battle inside her mind begins, I draw her to me, hold her against my chest. She fights at first, opening the scratches that barely have time to scab over from the previous night. I don't restrain her, but I do hold on to her. And then she settles and sleeps. Sometimes she cries. Just quiet, hopeless sobs. Those episodes don't last long, thank goodness. I don't think I could bear them if they did. Through it all, I just hold her.

I push my hand through my hair and scrub my face. Lois is right. I need to sleep. Tomorrow during the day. Right now, Mercedes is my priority.

"Go get some rest, Lois."

She nods. She's tired too. "You come get me if she needs me." Lois has moved into a guest room a few doors down. She lives in a cottage on the property but since the incident, she moved herself into the main house to be available at all hours.

"Judge," comes Mercedes's hoarse voice again. Lois disappears and I go to her.

"I'm here."

I meant what I said. I will watch over her. Always.

She exhales, settles into sleep once she hears me.

Another week has passed like this. The doctor took the IV out this morning and we're slowly easing her off the sedatives which he prescribed to help her sleep and get the rest she needs to heal. The damage my brother did was more mental than physical. I'm not sure that's a good or bad thing.

Lois and I have woken her to eat what little she'll eat. Mostly a few spoonful's of soup. During the day she sleeps more peacefully than she does at night. We leave the curtains open, let the light in. It seems to calm her. Reassure her.

At night, though, it's different. Like the darkness settles inside her. I wonder what hell traps her in the dreams that come during the small hours when she lashes out to fight invisible beasts.

During the day I sit in the chair beside the bed and watch over her. I work a little, although I can't concentrate on anything but her. At every sound, no matter how slight, she draws all my attention.

As dark descends now, I wait for the cycle to begin anew. To watch as she becomes restless, lines etching the smooth skin of her forehead, her hands clenching and unclenching to fight off her demons.

Demons. She has several. Her father the first. I

wonder if Santiago is one for the fact that he gave her to me. Cast her out of his home. Out of his life.

And when she came to be in my keeping, I became the third demon to torment her. My own desire became her undoing. My selfish want of her.

And there is now a fourth. My brother.

How safe have I kept her in my home? Not at all. First Miriam. And what did I do but call Mercedes a liar and punish her? Then my brother. And throughout it all, me. From the very beginning, the very first night she arrived. How safe has she been from me?

I go into the bathroom to wash my face. I look a wreck. My cheeks have hollowed out. The skin around my eyes is shadowed. The bruise along my jaw is nearly gone, the cut on my cheekbone that required stitches will leave a mark. Not that I care. Mercedes took the brunt of his rage, although, thankfully, her injuries weren't as bad as I expected. He could have done worse. He held back. Which is the one thing that may save his life.

That's not true though. It's not the one thing. There's a reason my grandfather paid him off. If the truth had come out that Theron wasn't of Montgomery blood, it would have shamed the old man. Tainted the family name. Theron knew how important this was to our grandfather and used that fact against him. Because being a Sovereign Son, he is protected by IVI's laws. To murder

Theron would have meant a death sentence to my grandfather. It will mean one to me.

But it doesn't excuse what he did. He will pay.

Mercedes makes a sound and I hurry back into the bedroom. I strip down to my briefs and put on the folded pair of pajama pants Lois left on the foot of the bed, then lift the blanket to climb in beside her.

"No!" she starts. It's always the same.

"Shh. You're safe, Mercedes. It's me. It's Judge."

With effort she opens her eyes to peer at me, but then closes them again.

I settle in beside her and the bed dips. Her body curls into mine. I cover both of us with the blanket and wrap an arm around her.

She pushes against my chest momentarily. When I don't budge, her fingernails dig in. Although Lois cut them down when she saw my chest so she can't do as much damage.

"You can turn me black and blue, little monster, but I won't leave you," I whisper against her ear, then kiss her temple. "Sleep now. You're safe."

She mutters something then settles down. An owl hoots outside. I hold on to her. My eyelids feel heavy but I fight to keep them open because if I sleep, I'll have my own nightmare. I'll relive that night, going over it again and again to understand something I can't understand.

Light pours into the room. I wake to the clicking of a door and the smell of coffee. When I open my eyes, I see the steaming mug Lois must have just left.

I slept. A full night according to the clock which tells me it's a little after nine in the morning.

Mercedes is curled into me, dark hair fanned out over my chest, her chin against my shoulder. One hand is laid flat over my heart. I hold my breath for a moment when I see that. It's the same every morning. And so is my reaction to it.

My arm is beneath her neck and she's so warm and soft tucked into me like she is that I don't want to move.

But I need to get out of the bed and dressed before she wakes up. I don't want her to startle to find me beside her half naked. The memory of what happened between us prior to the incident is still very clearly etched into my brain and even given what's come to pass, I need to take care that we don't slip back into that other impossible situation.

I slide my arm out from under her and slip out of the bed. I wash my face then brush my teeth. I need to shave, too, but those things are still in my own bathroom. When I return to the bedroom, I'm surprised to see Mercedes awake and trying to sit up.

We both freeze for a moment, staring at each other. Her gaze moves over me, taking in my naked torso, the pajama pants. My bare feet. By the time she meets my eyes again, she's steeled herself and I can't read her.

"What are you doing in here?" she asks, her voice hoarse from not having spoken for so long.

"Let me help you."

"I don't need your help."

"You do." I go to her, adjust the pillows. I'm careful not to touch her and grit my teeth when she winces, hissing through her teeth as she sits up against them. She looks at her arm, the bandage on the back of her hand where the IV was connected. There's a tiny bruise where the needle had gone in.

"Where are my pills?" she asks, glancing at the empty nightstand.

"After breakfast," I tell her. It's aspirin, just a low dose of aspirin.

"I need them."

"After breakfast, Mercedes." I walk toward the chair where my clothes from yesterday have been folded. I pull on my sweater.

"I need the pills. It hurts."

"You'll get them after breakfast. The doctor said it's time to wean you off."

Her forehead furrows. "It's just a week ago."

I shake my head. "Two weeks and a day now."

"Two weeks?"

I nod.

She looks upset by this. Upset and confused.

"Theron is gone. He won't hurt you again."

At the mention of his name her eyes fill up and she clenches the sheet, shifting beneath it. How much does she remember? How much of what he did to her. Of what I did to him.

"Where's Lois?" she asks and I'm relieved.

"Would you like me to go get her?"

She nods, looks away from me like she can't quite hold my gaze.

I bow my head and walk out of the room to find Lois just coming up the stairs. "She wants you."

Lois stops when she sees my face but doesn't say anything. I wait by the door as Lois enters.

"Sweetheart," Lois sits on the edge of the bed and brushes Mercedes's hair from her face. Mercedes is obviously comforted by her, and I wonder about the affection she's had in her life. None from her father, that I know. Was her mother affectionate? I know Antonia is a kind, sweet woman. But I also know Mercedes is fairly standoffish with her. "How are you feeling?"

She shrugs a shoulder. "I need to use the bathroom," she says in a low voice.

Lois nods, looks at me. I hurry back into the room to carry her, but Mercedes's eyes widen in panic, and I stop.

"It's okay," Lois says. "I can't carry you. Judge needs to do that, okay?"

"Then I can walk."

"You can't. Not on your own," I say and go toward the bed although at a slower pace.

She pushes the covers off and tries to swing her legs over the edge as if to show she can, but she very clearly cannot.

"I won't hurt you," I say and lift her before she can refuse. She has no choice but to hold me and once we're in the bathroom I let Lois help her and step out. A few minutes later, the door opens, and I carry Mercedes back to the bed. She keeps her face averted.

"I'll get your breakfast. Give me just a few minutes." Lois says.

Mercedes turns her untrusting gaze to me, then nods to Lois. Once Lois is gone, Mercedes looks at my discarded pajamas then at me.

"Did you touch me?"

I'm surprised by the cold tone of her voice. The question itself. Truly taken aback. "No. Of course not. Mercedes, I would never—"

"Well, lucky me that one of the Montgomery brothers has found his moral compass."

I swallow that down. I deserve it and more.

"Did he?" she grits her teeth, eyes wet as she forces herself to hold my gaze. "Did he? I can't... remember everything."

"No." The doctor confirmed he hadn't sexually assaulted her.

She nods, pulls her knees up and looks down. I hear the relief in her shuddering exhale of breath. She wipes her eyes.

Lois is back then. She's holding a tray loaded with so much food I don't actually know how she carried it. It's clearly all of Mercedes's favorites.

"Here we are. I brought a little of everything, so you just choose what you like."

"My pills?" Mercedes asks, looking over the tray.

"I'll bring them to you after you eat something."

Lois hands her a cup of tea with honey. Mercedes takes it and sips.

"I'll come back after my shower," I say, and walk to the door when Mercedes doesn't ask me to stay. I'm almost in the hallway when she calls out my name. I stop, turn and wait.

"Where is he?" she finally asks after a long minute.

"Gone."

I don't say that I'm not sure where because when I went back to that wretched room after making sure Mercedes was going to be alright,

Theron was gone. All that was left was the bloody spot where his head had been. His car was gone, too. I can't say what he took as far as clothes or money because I hadn't been inside the South Cottage since I gave it to him, and I have no idea how he drove himself or if he did, but he hasn't been seen or heard from and Ezra Moore, the investigator I hired to find him, has found nothing.

"You never have to see him again, Mercedes."

She nods, turns her attention to the steaming cup in her hands.

4

JUDGE

I spend most of the day with Ezra Moore, a man I trust, who is now digging deeper into Theron's finances. Ezra has worked with me multiple times over the years. He handles all sorts of personal business I need handled outside of IVI. I have frozen Theron's accounts but was surprised at how little money he had left considering I just paid him a sizeable allowance when he moved into the South Cottage and swore to stay away from Mercedes.

At first, I'd assumed he'd withdrawn all he could when he ran but it doesn't look like that's the case. And now, as we dig deeper into the accounts he held when my grandfather was paying him, I'm wondering exactly what is going on.

Because a lot of money is gone. And the way he looked the night he hurt Mercedes wasn't right. I'm beginning to suspect there's something more complex and darker in my brother's life than I thought.

My mother, of course, claims to know nothing. Claims he couldn't have done what he did and that it must have been sexual play that got out of hand. Then she accused Mercedes of being to blame, using Theron to make me jealous, and claiming Theron was only confused as to what she wanted. I almost killed her then and there. Paolo was with me when I questioned her. If he hadn't been I'm not sure what I would have done.

She's been smart enough to keep to herself in her cottage in the weeks since and I'll be monitoring her comings and goings because I know one thing for sure. She'll cover for Theron. And it's just a matter of time until he needs money and he's in touch.

Late in the afternoon I make my way down to Royal Street where King George III flower shop is located.

King George III. I'm not sure how much more pretentious he can be. George Beaumont, or Georgie as Mercedes calls him, is the third George in his family but the play on the name for his shop irritates me.

I reel it in, though. I'm doing this for Mercedes. I need to give her this.

King George III is hard to miss. Its exterior is

candy pink, the door standing open, about a thousand multi-colored roses serve as a canopy over the entrance of the trendy shop and even before I enter, I'm overwhelmed by the sheer amount of color and sweet scent pouring out of the place.

From inside, a man laughs, and it grates on my nerves. I'm sure that's Georgie.

I try not to scowl as two customers walk out, a middle-aged woman and her daughter I'd guess. They're holding a bouquet and from the bits and pieces of conversation I hear, he's providing the flowers at the younger woman's wedding.

Once they're gone, I enter the shop, which is not big but so overfull it would be too much anywhere else. The way *Georgie* has it laid out, though, I admit, it's well done if a little much. Like a vomiting of color all around and above me with the drying flowers hanging upside down in various shades. When I reach the front of the shop, I find Georgie himself standing behind the counter studying me.

"Welcome to King George III," he says with not quite the warmth he showed the two women who just left.

"Thank you," I say, studying him, too. He looks different in person than he does in his photos. I guess I'd made up a personality based on his text exchanges with Mercedes but he's more serious here. Or maybe he's just more serious now that I'm in the shop and he senses something.

"Can I help you?"

"I'd like some flowers."

He raises his eyebrows. "Well, you're in the right place," he says and checks his watch. "But I am closing early this afternoon so if you can let me know the occasion or if you have something special in mind, I can help you."

I hadn't thought about this.

"A budget, perhaps?" he asks when I don't answer right away. His eyes move over my bespoke suit.

That's when I glance at the framed photo on the counter. On top is a handwritten note asking, 'have you seen me?' with an arrow pointing down to Mercedes's smiling face.

I peer closer. It's a smile I haven't seen. Not that I've seen her smile much. Maybe she does more of that in her other life. I feel that thought like a physical thing. A tightening of my chest. She's standing between Georgie and her friend, Solana. They must be at some kind of party from their dress and Mercedes, for as gorgeous as she looks, is definitely more than a little tipsy. The three of them have their arms around each other and Solana is bent double laughing as Georgie kisses Mercedes's cheek, he, too, laughing too hard at something.

"All proceeds from purchases this week will go toward finding her," he says somberly. He picks up the framed photo and dusts something off it, then sets it down and looks at me. "Our friend in the middle is missing. Haven't seen or heard from her in two months."

"Is it possible she doesn't want to be seen or heard from?"

"No, it's not." He looks at her photo when he continues. "I think someone hurt our beautiful, sweet girl."

His words repeat in my head. *Someone hurt our beautiful, sweet girl.*

"It's the only explanation," he continues. "And every time we try to put up an ad or file a missing person's report, poof, it disappears. Like fucking voodoo."

I clear my throat.

"Someone powerful doesn't want her found. That's what I think. But we're holding a candlelight vigil this weekend. And every news channel will stream it live. Then let's see the bastards try to stop us."

"A candlelight vigil?"

"You should come." He looks me over again. "Although I'm not sure you're the type."

"What type is that?"

"Never mind. Tell me the occasion and I'll make you a gorgeous bouquet."

"What kind of flowers does she like?"

"Who?"

"Mercedes."

He pauses and I realize my mistake. His gaze sharpens on me. He's trying to think back if he said her name.

"Roses. In every color but red."

"Hm. Then I'll take them."

"Them?"

"All the roses you have in every color but red."

"That's a lot of roses."

I take the black American Express out of my wallet. "Good."

He looks suspiciously at me but punches a number into the register. I'm sure he's marking up his roses but I don't care. I swipe the Amex and sign my name, then take a different card out of my wallet.

"You'll deliver them personally to this address tomorrow night. You and your friend, Solana Lavigne."

He reads my name on the card, my position, then meets my gaze. His is harder this time. Nothing friendly left in it.

"I'll see you tomorrow, Georgie." I turn to leave, picking up a ready-made bouquet of the roses I just bought and walking out of the shop before he can say another word and before I can understand what I just did.

When I get home, Lois tells me dinner is almost ready. I want Mercedes to eat downstairs with me tonight. We need to get back into a normal rhythm. I can't keep her locked up in her bedroom and she can't keep ignoring me.

I knock softly in case she's sleeping but when she doesn't answer I open the door. My heart immediately drops to my stomach when I don't see her, afraid of a repeat of what just happened. But then Mercedes emerges from the bathroom and stops dead when she sees me.

She's dressed in a loose-fitting, ankle-length dress and picks up the sweater that's lying on the foot of the bed and puts it on.

"Do you knock?"

"I did. You didn't hear me."

"Then wait until I do."

I clear my throat, see the red gash where the whip must have caught her wrist. Before I have a chance to speak, her gaze moves to the flowers and she must recognize the paper wrapping because she crosses the room, grabs them out of my hand, confirms where they're from and hugs them protectively to herself.

"What did you do?" She screams. "What the hell did you do?"

I hold my hands out, palms up. "I invited your friends to the house."

"You what?" Clearly not what she was expecting.

"I invited your friends."

"Here?"

"Here."

"Why?"

"Don't you want to see them?"

She watches me suspiciously. "What's your game?"

"There's no game, Mercedes."

"Then what do you want?"

I look down at the chipped pink polish on her toes. Not her usual shade of blood red. I recall Georgie's words. *Every color but red*. I'm slow to return my gaze to hers.

"I want to see you smile. Hear you laugh maybe," I say. It's probably one of the most honest things I've ever said to her. To anyone.

There's a moment of silence and I'm not sure where this is going. If she's going to burst into tears. If she's going to throw herself into my arms. But she does neither of those things.

"It's all about what you want, isn't it, Judge? You wanted to fuck me. You fucked me. But then you decided you didn't want me after all, so you locked me up. Literally. And when I tried to escape you, your brother decided to take what he wanted too.

Maybe it's all the Montgomery men and their wants. No. That's not right. It's all men and their wants. Their whims. And women are just pawns. At least within The Society."

She steps toward me, protecting her flowers from me.

"You want to see me smile? Hear me laugh. Once upon a time I would have given you that. Did you know that? I would have given you anything. But that time is past. You didn't want me and you can't change your mind anymore. So now you can want all you like. I will never smile for you. And if you ever hear me laugh, the instant I see your face that laugh will die. Because you know what I want, Judge? I want to be free of you. Of all of you!"

5

MERCEDES

I apply my crimson red lipstick with a shaky hand, feeling strangely at odds with the woman staring back at me in the mirror. I still recognize her beneath the makeup, but she feels like someone from another life.

The routine I used to fall into so easily every day, applying my armor before I stepped out into the world, now makes me feel like a stranger in my own skin. When Judge sent Lois to give me back my makeup bag this morning, I knew it wasn't out of the kindness of his heart. Neither is his agreement to let me see my friends. I would be a fool to believe that for even a second.

The reality of it is I'm his hostage, and this is a negotiation, much like everything else in my life. I have no doubts Georgie and Solana have been making a lot of noise about my absence, and The

Society won't like that. Judge has certainly let it be known that he doesn't either. Today isn't about allowing me to spend time with my friends. It's about showing proof of life to keep them quiet.

A deep wave of grief moves over me, and my lipstick clatters into the sink, smearing red across the white porcelain. Goddammit, I'm so sick of crying. I wave my hands in front of my face, forcing the tears back before they ruin the makeup I've spent the last twenty minutes applying. I can't do this. Not today.

Just when I think I've succeeded in pulling myself together, a door slams from somewhere down the hall, and it makes me jolt. My chest pulls tight, throat squeezing as my heart knocks against my rib cage at a frantic pace. A cocktail of hormones floods my body, and I have to grip the sink hard to keep from passing out.

It's just a fucking door, I tell myself as I close my eyes and drag in some steadying breaths. But even so, it takes me several minutes to come back to myself. And I hate that I've become so weak. The Mercedes De La Rosa I know never showed fear. She didn't startle over the slightest unexpected noise or jump whenever someone came into the room. She didn't cry for no reason at all, and she certainly didn't let a fucking man wound her pride.

I don't know what's happening to me, but I

know I don't like whatever it is. To make things worse, everyone is looking at me like I'm a delicate little doll, handling me with kid gloves to make sure I don't break.

Today will have to be different. I will need to make sure of it, for Solana and Georgie's sake. They need to see the Mercedes they know and love. They need to leave here with nothing less than confidence in my assurances I'm okay, for their own safety. I don't need Judge to remind me of that.

With a shuddered breath, I pick up the fallen tube of lipstick and cap it, returning it to my bag and zipping it up. Then I stare at my reflection as my fingers move to the knot of my robe, lingering with hesitation. I haven't looked at any of the marks other than the one still fading on my wrist. I haven't been brave enough. But I know if I want to return to myself, it's time to face it. I need to see the fresh scars left by another man's anger for me to bear for all of eternity.

I close my eyes and unknot the belt slowly, forcing the material off my shoulders until it slides over my body and pools at my feet. My legs feel far too stiff as I pivot, turning my head over my shoulder and sucking in a sharp breath before I force my eyes open.

A second passes, followed by another, and confusion melts over me as I examine the flesh I was certain would be forever ruined. Except, there is only one faint mark that's nearly healed, a light pink line across my left thigh. And I can't make sense of it. I don't understand.

My trembling fingers move over the skin for confirmation as I wonder if I'm hallucinating. But clearly, I'm not. I can feel nothing but smooth skin where I was convinced there were deep cuts. My mind drifts back to that night, and I shake as I recall the time that passed afterward.

They kept me drugged, but why? Was it for the pain, or something else?

"Oh." Lois's soft voice startles me, and when I meet her gaze in the mirror, I can see the concern etched into her features.

"I'm sorry," she whispers. "I didn't mean to—"

"There aren't any scars," I murmur dazedly.

She hesitates on the threshold of the bathroom, her empathetic eyes shining with the answer I didn't want to see.

"No," she says softly. "There aren't any new scars."

"So I was drugged because..." The words trail off when I can't bring myself to admit I lost my grip on reality.

"It was for your own protection and your peace of mind." Lois takes a careful step forward. "Judge didn't want you to suffer."

I trace the length of the faint pink line where

Theron used the cane. "How much of it was real?" I whisper. "How much was in my head?"

Lois comes to me, reaching down to grab my robe and gently drapes it over my shoulders before she turns me to meet her gaze.

"Sometimes the past has a way of dragging us back," she explains delicately. "And sometimes, we're trapped between that past and the present. The pain you felt was real, Mercedes. You didn't imagine that."

I understand what she's telling me. It was real to me, no matter what it looked like on the outside. Because in my fragile state, I was trapped in a memory. A time when my wounds seemingly wouldn't heal. When the split skin twisted and snarled and embedded itself so deep into my psyche, it won't ever let me go.

"You must think I'm insane." I bring my fingers to my temples and press, hoping to keep the emotion at bay.

"No." Lois's voice is firm, but kind. "I think you've been through hell, sweetheart. And what happened to you isn't any less traumatic just because it didn't leave visible scars this time. Some of our most painful experiences are the ones that leave scars nobody can see. That doesn't make them any easier to live with."

"Thank you," I murmur. "For being so nice to me."

"You deserve nothing less." She squeezes my shoulder. "Don't forget that, dear."

It would be tempting to argue that notion, but Lois is too sweet to see anything other than good in the people around her. And for that I can be grateful, even if I don't truly deserve it.

"Now." She offers me a lighthearted smile. "Let's get you dressed, shall we?"

JUST A LITTLE PAST SIX O' clock, my bedroom door creaks open, alerting me to Judge's presence. I don't have to look up from my book to know it's him. The energy changes the moment he appears, as if he sucks all the oxygen from the room. But when I bookmark my page and glance up at him, it would seem, for only a moment, I might possess some of the same magic too.

He's staring at me with unmistakable heat in his eyes as they take in the red pencil dress that hugs every inch of my body. I can see I've caught him off guard, but I don't know why he'd expect anything less. This is the Mercedes he's always known before he decided to strip me bare.

His gaze trails over the square neckline, over the gentle curves of my cleavage, and down my hips all the way to my black Louis Vuitton heels.

He scrubs a hand over his jaw, muttering a curse before his gaze darts back to mine.

"You look beautiful," he says.

I don't reply. I'm not in the business of thanking men for compliments after they've discarded me. But there is something about the tension in Judge's body that sets me on guard. I noticed it this morning during our brief interaction when he reappeared. His mind was somewhere else, and I couldn't help wondering where exactly that was.

I heard him leave late last night as I lay in my bed, staring at the wall with my back to him. He's still sleeping in my room, which I don't understand. But I suppose he needs to make sure I don't off myself in his care and ruin his precious reputation.

That's what I choose to believe because he's shown me who he is, and he showed me again last night. When his phone received an incoming text long past reasonable business hours, he didn't hesitate to answer it before he got up and left.

I stood by the window and watched his car disappear down the long driveway, wondering who it was he was going to see. Which courtesan has so captured his attention that she is able to call him to her in the middle of the night?

As much as I hate to admit it, the reality still chokes the air from my lungs. It burns my skin and makes me wish I could forget the feeling of his hands on my body. The feeling of him inside me. I gave something to him I can't ever give anyone else, and he chose to stomp all over it.

"Your friends are here," he informs me. "We're going to have dinner together."

I nod and rise on shaky legs, forcing some steel into my backbone as I walk to join him. When I do, he halts me at the door with his fingers on my chin, tipping it up so I'm forced to look at him.

"No games tonight, Mercedes."

He doesn't state it like a threat, but I know it is. I can see he's not in the mood, and quite frankly, neither am I. When it comes to Solana and Georgie, I'm not about to do anything stupid to put them at risk. He would understand that if he truly knew anything about me.

"No games," I sigh my agreement.

He nods, releasing my face only to press his hand to my lower back and guide me out into the hall. We walk together in silence, both of us seemingly lost in our own thoughts. A nervous flutter stirs in my belly as we near the sitting room, and I'm praying for the strength to hold it together when I see my friends. I'm excited and anxious, though you couldn't tell from my stone-cold exterior.

When we turn the corner and Judge guides me inside the room, Solana and Georgie both jump up from the sofa to greet me with equal gasps of shock and relief.

"Oh, my God." Solana wails as she closes the distance between us, dragging me into her arms as she begins to sob. "I thought you were dead, Mercedes!"

I don't have a moment to speak before Georgie wraps his arms around me too, and I'm engulfed by the two of them. Despite my best efforts, their tears spur my own, and I find myself choking on breaths of air before Judge seems to sense my despair and clears his throat behind us.

"Shall we sit down?"

They both release me reluctantly, Solana holding me at arm's length as her eyes move over me. I don't miss the challenge Georgie shoots Judge with his gaze as he strokes my arm and squeezes my hand in his.

"Are you okay, love?" he asks.

"Where have you been?" Solana demands. "We've been worried sick."

My eyes move over them, Solana in her long, witchy black dress with silver bangles adorning her arms. She's as beautiful as ever. Even as she glares at Judge with her bright green eyes like she's taking a mental picture for the voodoo doll she'll make in his likeness. And then there's Georgie, come to rescue me in his finest suit, a navy-blue affair with a patterned pocket square. They have such a calming, protective presence it makes me feel like myself again, even if it is only for just a moment. God, I have missed them so much.

"Mercedes?" Solana gives me a gentle squeeze, and I realize I still haven't spoken.

I open my lips, but nothing comes out. That's when Judge takes it upon himself to intervene, branding his hand around my waist possessively before he pulls me back against him. It's unexpected, and when I turn to look up at him, his eyes flare as he brushes his fingers over my jaw in an obvious display of ownership.

I don't have to guess who it's for. There's a palpable tension between my friends and him, but most notably, the biggest threat he perceives is Georgie. It's such a ridiculous notion I almost want to laugh, but I decide to let him make a fool of himself instead by pissing imaginary circles around me.

"I come bearing drinks." Lois interrupts the moment, dissolving some of the tension as she hands out a wineglass to each of us, with the exception of Judge, who doesn't take anything.

I find it rather odd but shove my curiosity aside as we all take our seats. Georgie and Solana return to the sofa, and Judge keeps me close to his side on the chaise opposite them.

"So?" Georgie arches a brow at me. "Are we going to get any explanation?"

I don't miss the way his eyes dart to Judge's hand around my back in question. That question feels like a *what the hell are you doing, Mercedes?*

"I'm so sorry I haven't been in contact," I begin, trying to gather my thoughts as I speak.

I didn't really have a plan for how I was going to explain my absence, but I don't think it matters. There's nothing I can really say to justify it. All I can hope is that I convince them I'm okay, and they don't need to worry about me. This is how things are handled in IVI. Society business stays in The Society.

"Tell us what's going on," Solana pleads.

"I—" My voice fractures slightly before Judge's fingers press into me.

"Mercedes was involved in an incident," Judge supplies for me. "For her protection, she needed to come stay with me, and she's been under my care. It's for her own safety."

"What the hell does that mean?" Georgie narrows his gaze at him.

"We want a word with Mercedes in private," Solana demands.

I look at Judge in a silent plea. He knows they aren't going to take his word, and I need him to trust that I can handle this. He's only making things worse right now by trying to manage the situation for me.

His arm stiffens around me as he realizes what

I want, but reluctantly, he nods and rises to his feet.

"I'll go check on dinner," he grunts before shooting Georgie a warning look. And then, to top things off, he leans down and brushes his lips against my forehead in a gentle kiss.

It shocks me so much I can't seem to speak when he releases me. I'm still staring after him in confusion when he leaves the room, and it's only the sound of Solana's voice that brings me back to the present.

"Mercedes, what the hell is going on?" She comes to my side, Georgie squeezing in on the other. "Who is that guy?"

"He's my... guardian," I try to explain.

Both of them frown. I don't know how to navigate this situation. I've never needed to describe something like this to an outsider. Everyone in The Society understands the rules, but the rest of the world doesn't. It isn't something they can wrap their heads around. It will take a delicate balance of giving them enough information to satiate their concerns but not too much to endanger them.

"You're twenty-five years old," Georgie says. "Why would you need a guardian?"

"It's... complicated," I grumble. "But this is how things work in my world. I know it's hard to understand but please try. It's Judge's job to protect me. He wasn't lying about that."

Her Rebellion 57

"Protect you from what?" Solana asks.

I dip my gaze to the floor, recalling the reason I ended up here in the first place. "From myself, mostly."

They glance at each other, and Georgie's hand squeezes mine. "Are you in danger?"

"Do you want to be here?" Solana adds.

"I'm not in danger," I assure them, though nothing has ever felt like more of a lie. "And... I'm safe here."

They aren't fooled by my vague assertions, and it shows.

"I just don't understand this," Georgie growls. "Something isn't right. We want you to come back with us. Please, Mercedes."

"I can't do that." I offer him a shaky smile. "I'm sorry, but—"

"Are you in the mafia?" Solana whispers, her eyes wide. "Is that it?"

I can't help but laugh at her observation, but she doesn't share my amusement.

"What else am I supposed to think?" she hisses quietly. "You're so guarded about your life. Your family. We realized after you disappeared how little we actually know about you. Then this guy shows up at Georgie's shop, throwing around his wealth, and gives us this address with a mysterious invitation. And this place... it's like a fucking fortress. None of it adds up."

My eyes drift to the vases of roses around the room, and a strange warmth creeps over my chest. I know there are more important things to focus on, but I can't understand why Judge would buy all of those.

"Does this have something to do with that weird tattoo on the back of your neck?" Georgie asks.

I stiffen at the mention of it, and they don't miss it.

"It means something," Solana agrees. "But you've never explained it."

"Look." I squeeze each of their hands in mine. "I am so sorry I made you worry about me. I truly didn't mean to, and I feel terrible about that. If I could have contacted you, I would have. I've missed you both every single day, and it means so much to me to know that you care. But I can assure you I'm safe, and I'm not in the mafia."

"Semantics." Georgie rolls his eyes. "Whatever it is they call themselves these days. It's the only thing that makes sense. Don't insult us by lying to us."

"I'm not trying to insult you," I whisper. "I'm trying to protect you."

They both frown, and I know that was the wrong thing to say. I work quickly to try to correct it.

"There's a lot in my life you don't know about,

Her Rebellion

and I can't explain. I wish I could, but it's not safe for you to know these things. What I can promise you is that I'm okay here, and I just need to stay under Judge's protection until things blow over."

"When will that be?" Solana asks, the evidence of her hurt clearly written on her face.

I hate that I'm doing this to them. I hate that I can't be honest with them about The Society, but it really is for their own safety. I don't trust that Judge isn't going to punish them if I make one wrong move.

"I don't know just yet," I admit. "But I swear to you, the moment I do, you'll be the first to hear from me."

"No." Georgie shakes his head. "We need a line of communication with you. We aren't leaving here until we have that."

"We're not waiting in the dark," Solana agrees.

I swallow painfully, trying to figure out how I'm going to tell them that's not possible, when Judge interrupts from behind us.

"She has a new phone," he tells them. "You can text or call her on that number. I'll give it to you before you leave."

I glance back at him, my eyes searching his, but I can't make out the motivation behind his concession. It feels too good to be true, but there is no sign of deception on his face.

"I don't understand why she hasn't had it this

whole time," Solana mutters. "But whatever. If you miss even one of my calls or texts, I'm coming to check on you. Let that be clear."

Judge looks less than pleased with her threat, but he simply jerks his chin in agreement before gesturing to the dining room.

"Dinner is ready."

6

MERCEDES

With the assistance of a few more glasses of wine, we fall into a much less stilted conversation during dinner. Judge is mostly a silent observer from his seat, his fingers trailing over my shoulder as my friends pepper me with questions and then catch me up on the latest happenings in their own lives.

They explain how they've been trying to bring attention to my disappearance but have been blocked at every turn. Their inferences don't escape my notice. If they didn't believe I was connected to some type of powerful organization before, this seems to confirm it.

"I mean how the hell do the police just make something like that disappear?" Solana questions. "Then there are the lawyers. What kind of lawyer turns down money? And don't get me started on the private investigators we hired. One of them just seemed to evaporate into thin air."

I dart a glance at Judge, and he squeezes my shoulder in a silent warning that now isn't the time to talk about that. He can't seem to stop sizing up Georgie, and I know that's what's been on his mind throughout dinner as he observes us.

"How is business?" I ask Georgie and Solana, trying desperately to change the subject.

"Fine." Solana waves her hand dismissively. "We've been too focused on you to worry about that."

"When can we see you again?" Georgie meets Judge's gaze as he directs the question to me. "Outside of this house. Everyone misses you at aerial class."

Judge's fingers stop moving against my shoulder, and I hate that I'm waiting for him to speak, but there's no point in trying to supply an answer myself.

"She can come as soon as she's feeling up to it," he says. "I'll take her personally."

This really seems to irk Georgie, but Solana is trying to read between the lines.

"What does that mean, when you're feeling up to it?"

"It's nothing." I shrug half-heartedly. "I've just been a little under the weather."

Again, Judge's hand tenses on me, and then he gently massages my shoulder as if he's trying to give me some sort of silent apology. Georgie and Solana don't miss it, their eyes lasering in on the action.

"Are you guys together?" Solana asks.

"No," I answer at the same time Judge says, "Yes."

I glare at him, and he shrugs. This interaction only seems to confuse Solana and Georgie more.

"It's nothing serious," I tell them through clenched teeth. "Judge doesn't do serious, isn't that right?" I shoot him a look that betrays my annoyance. "He can have his fun, and I can too."

The gentle stroke of his fingers turns to stone as he drags his palm to the nape of my neck and squeezes. I smile as Solana clears her throat awkwardly.

"Good, then I guess that means you can resume date nights with me," Georgie challenges.

Oh, shit.

I offer him a nervous laugh, but the tension radiating from Judge serves as a warning I need to wrap this up before he changes his mind about everything.

"Let's circle back to that another time." I force a yawn. "It's getting late, and I know we all have to be up early."

They both look dismayed by that statement, knowing I'm typically a night owl.

"What do you have to be up early for?" Solana asks.

"She has a long day of riding tomorrow," Judge supplies, his tone dripping with overt insinuation.

"Riding." Georgie scoffs.

"Yes." Judge looks at me, his gaze scorching. "She loves to ride."

Oh, God, this is getting out of hand.

I stand abruptly, tossing my napkin onto the table. "Yes, well… shall I walk you to the door?"

Reluctantly, Solana and Georgie rise from their seats.

"What about your number?" Georgie asks. "Can't forget that."

"No, we certainly can't." Judge grouses as he removes a slip of paper from his pocket and makes a point to hand it directly to Solana.

After that awkward standoff, they both begrudgingly thank him for dinner, and I walk them to the door as promised.

"Are you sure you're okay here?" Solana asks. "You can come with us."

"We can protect you too," Georgie assures me. "Whatever it is, we'll figure it out."

"I'm okay." I offer them both a grateful smile, warmed by their genuine concern for me. "But thank you for the offer. Don't forget to text me."

"Girl, I'm texting you before I even leave the driveway," Solana jokes. "And I wasn't kidding. If I don't hear from you, I'm coming back."

I nod. Even though I probably should tell her not to, I can't bring myself to do it.

"I love you guys," I whisper.

"We love you too." They squeeze me in another long hug, and after more quiet tears, I reluctantly usher them out the door, staring at them until Judge's presence behind me makes me shiver.

"You did well." He strokes my hair over my shoulder, his tone approving.

I pull away from him and turn around, crossing my arms as I glare at him.

"We're together, Judge? Really? Why would you tell them that?"

His silent response only irritates me further, and I think that's all I can expect from him, but then he surprises me.

"I don't like the way he looks at you."

"Oh, my God, you are such a fucking hypocrite." I laugh caustically. "As if you didn't tell me you're out every night with another woman. Do I need to remind you I don't belong to you? That isn't my purpose for being here. You don't fucking own me."

"Yes, I do," he growls.

Unbelievable. Seriously, un-fucking-believable. I turn to leave, and he grabs me by the wrist, dragging me back to him until my chest collides with his, and he tightens his hold on me, locking me in his arms.

"For now." He breathes the words as if he regrets them. "You belong to me."

"For now," I choke on my reply. "I belong to nobody. Least of all you."

He lowers his face to mine, trying to ensnare me in a kiss, and I jerk away, only for him to grab my jaw. He holds me in place, his lips hovering over mine, the heat between us an inferno I can't understand.

"I've been inside you." His words heat my lips as he palms my ass with his other hand. "Only me."

"Well, I hope you enjoyed it." I smile up at him callously. "Because it was the first and the last time."

"I enjoyed it very much." The words sound like a confession, and it confuses me. "I think you did too."

He presses his thigh between my legs, nudging them apart, and I try to shake my head in protest. "No."

"Yes." His fingers skate down to the hem of my dress, and then against my bare thigh. "Even now, you enjoy it."

I hate that he's right. I hate that my heart is

beating erratically and my stomach is fluttering, and I'm secretly wishing for more all while hating myself for it. But I made a promise, and I intend to keep it.

"I don't want sloppy seconds." I press my hands against his chest and shove hard, surprising him as he stumbles back slightly.

It gives me the time I need to put much-needed distance between us as I dart toward the stairs, running back to the safety of my room. But Judge isn't far behind. I can hear the clip of his shoes on the floor before his voice caresses my back.

"Mercedes."

I ignore him as I fling myself through the doorframe, nearly tripping on my heels in the process as I attempt to slam the door in his face. He catches it with his palm, stopping the weight easily before he shoves it back open.

"I fucking hate you," I snarl at him.

"So you've said." A soft smile curves his lips. "I'm glad to see you're feeling more like yourself."

He stalks toward me, and I move back, the predator and the prey.

"You can't have me," I tell him. "Stop trying."

"I do have you." He seizes me by the waist and holds me in an unyielding grasp, his words humming against my neck as he inhales me. "You just don't know it yet."

A feeble protest leaves my lips as he kisses me, rough and possessive. He's not handling me delicately anymore. And as much as I know I should stop this, I don't. Not even a little bit.

I moan as his tongue invades my mouth, and he drinks my shallow breaths like they own him. I want to believe it's true, even for a second.

"Judge," I plead, my nipples stabbing against my dress, my body aching for something I can't quite articulate.

"I know." He shoves my dress up over my hips and then hoists me up into his arms, carrying me over to the bed.

I'm somewhere between trying to find the will to argue and the need to give in when he sets me down on the edge of the mattress and kneels before me. And fuck, it's a beautiful sight to have this powerful man brought to his knees by his want for me. But the thought enters my mind, and I can't stop it. How many other women has he done this with? Who did he do this with last night?

"Judge," the protest leaves my lips as he slips my thong over my ass and slides it down over my legs, careful not to entangle it on my heels before he removes it.

His palms come to rest on my thighs, spreading me apart, and I know I need to stop this insanity. I dig my fingers into his hair and he groans, sending a cascade of sparks through my body. But I still can't forget.

"Tell me her name," I demand.

"Who?" He kisses his way up my thighs, dragging his nose along my skin and inhaling me deeply.

A breath blows through my lips, and I shake my head, trying not to let him distract me.

"The name of the courtesan you like to fuck."

He ignores me, continuing his sensual assault on my inner thighs as he slowly works his way inward, closer to the point of no return. But I can't let him. I need to hear him say it.

"Tell me." I tighten my grip on his hair. "Or so help me God, I will fuck every man who comes near me. I can assure you they won't be hard to come by. I doubt Paolo or Raul would refuse—"

"Goddammit, Mercedes." He nips at my thigh, and I yelp. "You drive me fucking crazy."

I try to shove him away, but he just yanks me closer, my ass hanging off the bed as he stares straight into the glistening depths of what he already knows belongs to him.

"There is no fucking courtesan," he growls. "Are you satisfied?"

"That's not what you told me—" A strangled sigh chokes my words as his tongue lashes against me. "Oh, God."

"Only I get this." He swirls his tongue around my clit, setting off fireworks in my belly. "Say it."

"You say it first," I pant. "Tell me why you're a such a fucking liar."

"You know why I said it," he growls. "And you believed it so easily. Fucking Christ, Mercedes. Why would I go to the Cat House when I can have you?"

His words warm me, even though they shouldn't. It doesn't make it any better. It proves he's not only a liar but also a hypocrite. Saying he can have me when all he does is push me away. Those thoughts are almost enough to douse me in cold reality, but Judge's hot tongue lashing against me makes everything else evaporate.

"Fucking say it," he commands. "This pussy belongs to me and only me."

"For now," I remind him, throwing the words he loves to use back in his face. "And only because of forced proximity."

Without warning, he yanks me against his face, burying his tongue inside me so deep I see a glimpse of heaven. Oh Jesus, he's good at that.

Any other smart-ass remarks I might have had are lost to the sound of him eating me out. He's feasting on me like a God, and I can't help but give in to it.

"Lawson," I whimper as he tortures me.

He freezes at the mention of his real name, and

I freeze too. Our eyes lock and something passes between us, but I can't identify it. It's too powerful. Too intense to be constrained by words.

"Say it again," he murmurs.

"Lawson," I repeat in a breathy voice.

"Yes." He hums his approval against me and returns to his task.

I squirm against him, closing my eyes and panting all while I hold him by the hair, a desperate heat crawling up the base of my spine and soaking into every nerve ending in my body. That heat builds and builds as I watch him devour me, and there's no question in my mind I'm hungry for more. So much more.

But all too soon, the pleasure reaches a peak, and I fall hard, jerking against his face as I come. Judge gives me one last lingering lick all the way up the seam of my pussy before he nuzzles his nose against me with a sigh. And I know he's trying to gather his strength. A war I refuse to fight him on anymore. If he wants to get on his knees and pleasure me, so be it. I won't beg him for his cock again no matter how much I might want it.

He leans back on his haunches, glances up at me, and licks my come from his lips. Heat curls in my chest, flushing my skin as my eyes move over him, hot and hungry. This thing between us feels out of control, and I know one of us needs to be smart enough to put a stop to it. So I decide it's going to be me.

"I want the phone you promised Solana and Georgie I would have."

He blinks, dragged away from his thoughts as I shove my dress back down and force myself to act unbothered by what just happened.

"It's already on the dresser," he tells me. "I delivered it this afternoon while you were napping."

My eyes move to the dresser, relief swelling when I see he's not lying.

"It's for your friends," he reiterates. "That number is only for them."

"And Santi," I challenge.

His eyes darken, and I don't like whatever it is I see in them, but I can't quite put my finger on it.

"Does he know what happened?" I ask. "Did he come to visit me?"

There's a long, heavy silence that passes before he sighs and shakes his head. Something in his demeanor changes completely, and I don't like it. I don't like it at all.

"Did you tell him?" I hate the edge of pain I can't hide in my voice.

"No," he answers solemnly. "I didn't."

"Of course not." I stand and try to skirt around him, desperate to lock myself in the bathroom. But he grabs my arm and stops me.

"I didn't tell him because something happened, Mercedes."

His words stop me cold, and I jerk my gaze back to him, dread curdling my stomach. "What do you mean?"

"It's Ivy," he says gently. "She had an accident. She's in the hospital, and they don't know if she's going to make it."

I stagger into him, nearly collapsing in his arms before he catches me with a muttered curse.

"How?" I croak. "How is that possible? I have to talk to him. I have to... oh, God. Is the baby okay?"

Judge gives me an uncertain glance. "I don't know. There's a lot we still don't know. They're trying to figure it out. But Santiago isn't in the frame of mind to answer those questions."

A sharp ache pierces my chest, expanding outward as I come to understand the gravity of the situation. I don't like Ivy. I don't want to like her, at least. But there is one thing I can't deny. My brother loves her. He sacrificed his revenge for her, forsaking our father and brother to have his own family with the enemy. I hated him for it. I resented her even more. But right now, I can feel his pain as if it were my own. As if I can finally understand what it might be like for him to have those things snatched away so coldly. He can't go through that kind of loss again. I know he won't survive it.

"She has to be okay," I whisper, true regret settling over me for the first time since I began my campaign of torment against her. "She has to."

"I know." Judge wraps me in his arms, brushing his palm over the length of my back. "I know, sweetheart."

7
JUDGE

A few days later, I'm stepping out of the shower when my phone rings. It's Santiago. I wrap a towel around my hips and pick it up.

"Santiago."

Silence on the other end.

"How is Ivy?" I ask.

"Stable. But no change. Nothing. She won't wake up."

I hear agony in my friend's voice. Hear the torment of guilt and powerlessness.

"Nothing," he says more quietly.

"It's early yet. Her body has been under a great deal of stress. I'm sure—"

"Nothing is sure, Judge. Nothing."

It's despair now.

"Give her time."

"My sister. I can't come right now. I know it's been a long time, but I can't."

"I told Mercedes what happened. She's worried about you. About Ivy."

He snorts.

"It's true, Santiago. And she'll understand if you can't visit. She's doing well. Be reassured in that."

"Thank you. I need…" He trails off. I've never heard him so distracted. Never seen him so beside himself like he was the night I saw him at the hospital beside his comatose wife.

"You go take care of your wife now. I'll take care of Mercedes. Call me if there's any change."

We disconnect and I set the phone aside to dry off. Abel ran his sister down. His pregnant sister. I think about my own family. My brother. Would he do the same to me? To Mercedes? To an extent he did. He hurt her to punish me. The only difference between Theron and Abel's actions is that Abel hates his sister as much as he hates Santiago. I don't think Mercedes matters much to Theron.

Is one of those things worse than the other?

I step out of the bathroom and am surprised to find Mercedes sitting on my bed dressed to ride texting someone on her new phone.

"Do you knock?" I ask, remembering her very question.

She wraps up what she's typing out, smiles at

whatever the response is probably from fucking Georgie, then deigns to look up at me.

"I did. You didn't hear."

"That so?" I walk past her, not missing how her eyes drop to the line of hair that disappears beneath the towel at my stomach. I grin. She's not immune to me, no matter how much she wants to believe she is. I make my way to the closet.

"You took a long shower. What were you doing in there?"

I pull on a pair of briefs, then my riding pants, take a button-down off the hanger, and put it on. I approach her as I fold the cuffs. "Jerking my dick to thoughts of you on your knees sucking me off." I brush past her. Her nipples scrape my arm through her blouse, and I suppress a groan of need.

I've eaten her pussy out night after night, and I'm not complaining, but jerking myself off in the shower is getting a little old. She's trying to prove a point and make me believe it's only about getting off. Like a man, she's quick to get dressed when she's done without giving a fucking thought to me or the state I might be in.

But I see how she looks at the swell of my neglected dick in my riding pants. It's just a matter of time.

"I will never kneel for you again, Judge," she says too late.

I push silver links through my cuffs, then turn to button my shirt as I study her. "Never say never, Mercedes. You don't want to tempt the gods."

"I mean it. Never is never. It'll just be you and your hand for the foreseeable future. Until you give me away that is."

I grit my jaw. She knows exactly which buttons to push.

"And when I fail a virginity test—"

"You won't fail. I'll see to that."

"What does that mean?"

"It means you don't have to worry about that."

"Like you'll pay someone off? And what do I do on my wedding night? Squeeze ketchup on the sheets?"

I stop listening at wedding night and pull on my boots. She's trying to provoke me. I look her over and nod. She's almost back to herself. She still jumps at sudden loud noises, and there are moments I witness her panic when we're alone, and she deems me a threat. We'll get there, though.

I have noted how she hasn't worn makeup apart from a little lip gloss since the night her friends were over. I haven't taken her makeup away, but she just hasn't put it on.

"Ready?"

She purses her lips in irritation but nods and slips her phone into her pocket. I set my hand on her lower back and guide her out of my room and through the house. We walk side by side to the stables. The morning air is crisp. A fog has settled over the grounds, making for strange but beautiful views.

"Was that Santi you were talking to?" she asks too casually. She's worried, though. I hear it.

I nod.

"Any change?"

"No."

We reach the stables, and she goes to Temperance's stall. She keeps her back to me as she greets the horse, her high ponytail swinging. "Does he blame me?"

"Of course not. You had nothing to do with what happened to Ivy."

I go to her and saddle her horse. I know she hates that I help her, but she's going to have to get used to it. While I secure the saddle, she bridles Temperance. When she doesn't respond, I turn her to face me and tilt her chin up, forcing her to meet my eyes.

"What happened to Ivy wasn't your fault. You know that, right?"

She shrugs a shoulder but can't quite hold my gaze.

"Mercedes."

"Judge." She rolls her eyes and pushes past me to mount her horse. She moves with ease and assurance, and it helps that the horse likes her. "Can we go already?"

I nod and glance at the horse I'd bought for Theron. She's smaller than Temperance. I think of my brother. Of the calls my mother has been receiving that are disconnected almost as soon as they connect. And I don't tell Mercedes that when I think of him, I think of the boy I knew before his twenty-fifth birthday. Because he's in trouble. The things Ezra has turned up leave no doubt.

"I'll go without you if you can't be bothered," Mercedes says.

"You'll do no such thing." I get Kentucky Lightning ready, and we ride for a long time that morning. Long enough to watch the sun burn off the fog racing each other, testing each other's skill. And in spite of herself, I do see Mercedes smile. She even laughs before she catches herself. I don't comment.

"Are you trying not to take me by that outbuilding?" she asks me as we circle back to the stables the long way around.

"Are you in a hurry to get to the house? I thought you'd enjoy more time outside."

"Tell me the truth, Judge."

"I don't want you upset."

"I won't be upset. You all have to stop treating me with kid gloves. I'm stronger for what happened."

"It's okay to be fragile sometimes."

"You mean weak."

"I mean fragile. It'll take time for the trauma—"

"There's no fucking trauma," she snaps and clicks her tongue. Temperance gallops off as Mercedes guides her in exactly the direction I was trying to avoid.

"For fuck's sake." I go after her, catching up and leaning over to take her reins and at least slow Temperance down. "Take it easy."

She snatches the reins back into her gloved hands, and we ride in tense silence toward the outbuilding that houses the punishment room. Once we reach it, she dismounts.

"I want to see it."

"It's locked. I don't have the key."

"Liar. Besides, there was no lock. He broke it."

"And you think I didn't fix it?"

She walks to the mouth of the building and enters. I dismount and follow her, using the flashlight on my phone to guide us. I show her the padlocked door.

"Satisfied?" I ask.

She looks up at me, her face mostly hidden in the shadows. "What was it? Before?"

I study her. Remember the trust she'd talked about what feels like an eternity ago. When she trusted me with her secret.

"We called it the punishment room."

Worry creases her forehead.

"My grandfather. He was, well, let's just say he ruled with an iron fist."

"Not your father?"

"No. My father was gentle. Which Grandfather found weak." I move to walk out of the cave, but she puts a hand on my arm to stop me. I turn to her, and in the light of my phone's flashlight, her eyes shift to the scar Theron left on my cheek. She reaches a hand up to touch it, fingers light. It's the first time she's touched me in, fuck, I can't remember how long. Apart from pulling my hair when my face is buried between her legs, she avoids my touch.

"Theron said something."

I swallow because I don't trust myself to speak. Not the way my heart is beating as her fingers make their way down my cheek and to my mouth, hovering there before she drops her arm to her side.

"When I cried out, he said that it could always be worse. He said that he's not the monster. That I have no idea what you're capable of."

I draw in a tight breath. The air in here seems thinner. I need to burn it down and leave only ashes. Because this building, it's like a fucking black hole of time that still manages to trap me and reach its claws into my present.

"What did he mean, Judge?"

I open my mouth to answer but my phone rings then, interrupting us, breaking into the moment. I see that it's Ezra. "I need to take this." I walk out toward the sunlight and answer, grateful for the call because I'm not sure I'm ready to answer that question.

"Judge, you need to come."

"What?" My heart thuds.

"I'm sending you my location now."

"You found him."

"He's in bad shape. They're working on him now, but you need to hurry."

I look at Mercedes, who is watching me. "I'll be right there."

Mercedes rolls her eyes as I disconnect. "Saved by the bell. Who's Ezra Moore?" she asks. She must have read my phone's screen.

"Come—"

"Who did he find?" she asks tightly.

"I'll get you back to the house."

She opens her mouth to argue, but I continue.

"Raul will take you to visit your friends for lunch," I say, deciding it on the spot. Because she knows exactly who he found, and I need a distraction.

Not bothering to wait for her permission, I grip her by the waist and hoist her up onto Temperance's back before mounting my own horse and riding back, anxious as my phone dings with the location, which, at a quick glance, tells me is a motel about two hours out of town.

"Judge," Mercedes says when I leave her once we're in the house.

"I need to go, Mercedes."

"It's your brother. You're going to see him."

"It's not like you think."

"No? How is it then?"

"We'll talk later. I need to go."

"I won't talk later."

I sigh, but I can't fix this now. If Ezra said it's bad, it's bad.

I DRIVE myself to the address Ezra sent, and when I pull up to the door, I see Ezra's car and one other. Neither looks like they belong here. Someone peers out of their motel room as I park my Audi and hurry to knock on the door. I didn't want to bring the Rolls in case anyone recognized it.

"Judge," Ezra says, opening it right away and stepping aside to let me take in the scene.

"Jesus." The room has been destroyed. Every glass surface shattered. Every piece of furniture splintered. The bed leans on broken legs. And on the disgusting blanket lying in a stain I'm sure is his own blood is my brother. My barely conscious brother who is almost unrecognizable. His face has been beaten so badly that both eyes are slits, the skin around them black and blue. His lip is cut, and blood has dried on his chin. His neck. His shirt has been ripped open, and what looks like cigarette burns mark almost the entirety of his chest. His feet are bare, and I'm pretty sure that dark spot on his jeans is dried piss.

The doctor who is cleaning a wound gives some instruction to his assistant. She nods and gets what he needs out of the medical bag. Theron already has an IV in his arm.

On the broken nightstand and lying on the floor are traces of white powder and a used needle.

"Is that...?" I start, but Ezra answers before I can finish.

"Cocaine."

It's what I suspected the night I found him in the punishment room. He was high.

"We've managed to stabilize him," Ezra says. "He's lucky we got here when we did."

"What the fuck happened?" I snap.

Theron groans at the sound of my voice. He turns his head, and I see how much it costs him.

"He was overdosing. The hotel manager called the local police. Luckily, I know the woman manning the desk there. She recognized his description. I sent my own doctor over. He was able to reverse the overdose."

"He'll be okay?"

"Yes."

"Good," I say, more relieved than I expect to feel.

"And I've already paid the manager. It'll all be kept quiet."

I nod, but that's not what I'm thinking about now. I step closer to the bed. "Who beat him?" Because I didn't do this.

The nurse working with the doctor cuts away his jeans. Theron hisses through his teeth. I see why. Because as the denim is pulled away from his thighs, the sliced, shredded skin comes into view. Whoever did this wanted to deliver maximum pain.

Ezra shakes his head as I take in the damage. "A dark SUV was seen speeding off the grounds. The manager had received a complaint from one of the nearby rooms about noise."

"Jesus, Theron."

I don't expect him to answer, but he gurgles something I can't quite make out.

"He's pretty out of it," Ezra says.

"We can move him as soon as I get these dressed," says the doctor.

Ezra nods, then turns to me. "I'm guessing you don't want to take him to a Society hospital."

"Correct."

"You can house him at your clinic?" he asks the doctor.

The doctor looks at me, and I know what he's seeing. A big fat payday. "I'll have to clear out my patients."

"That's fine. Do what you need to do," I tell him. "The SUV?" I ask Ezra.

"I've got a partial plate, but it won't be easy to track."

"Did he do this himself?" I ask, gesturing to the band around his arm and the needle on the floor.

"I don't think so. He was tied down when we got here," Ezra says. "And he doesn't have tracks. A regular user would have tracks. My guess is the coke was his, but whatever was in that needle wasn't."

I look at his arms, at the strips of bloody clothing. They used his shirt to tie him down. "Probably owed someone money."

"That would be my guess, considering what I have learned recently. My car is in the lot. Let's continue our conversation outside," Ezra says, glancing at the doctor. We step out, closing the door partially behind us. "I was going to courier these files to you, but then this call came in, so I brought them with me."

"What did you find?"

"I tracked down at least where some of the money went when he was in Europe. And finding him like this... The beating was inflicted to deliver pain but he'd have died of an overdose if the manager hadn't called it in. The intent was murder. I'm not even sure whoever was responsible cared about it looking like it, considering."

"Fuck." I follow Ezra to his car. He unlocks it remotely, then opens the trunk, where I see a small safe. He's nothing if not thorough.

"That bad?"

"It's not good." He unlocks the safe and hands me a sealed folder. "There's not much else you can do here. Go home and read what I sent you. We'll need to get ahead of it. If this was who I think it was, they tracked him from Europe to New Orleans and were pissed off enough to send soldiers. If they find out he survived, they'll come back to finish the job."

"How the fuck did I not know?"

"No one did. Not even your grandfather."

"I want to know the instant he's lucid."

"I'll take care of it," Ezra says.

"No calls. No disappearing acts. He's good at that."

"I got this, Judge. I'll call in private security."

"Thank you." I walk back into the motel room to look at my brother one last time. He seems to be asleep.

"Go," Ezra pushes.

I do.

I don't go home, though. I go to my office.

Mercedes is out on her lunch date with her

friends, and when Raul calls to tell me she wants to go shopping, I agree. It'll be a good distraction, and she may ask fewer questions later.

I expect to be home by dinner, but the information Ezra has gathered is worse than I would have imagined.

My brother has managed to get on the wrong side of the Italian mafia. He owes them money. A lot of it.

I spend most of the night reading through the thick file and reach out to my counterparts in that part of the world to learn as much about the family as possible. By the time I'm finished, I have a headache and am exhausted. It's after midnight when I get to the house, which is quiet. Raul is having a beer with Paolo in the kitchen. I pour myself a scotch and join them.

"How was she?" I ask Raul.

"Pleased with the shopping. She put a dent on your card, though."

"I'd expect no less." I swallow the scotch, smiling. I am guessing she bought her friends a whole new wardrobe compliments of me.

"Where is she now?"

The men shrug their shoulders. "Had dinner with Lois a little while ago. I guess she went up to bed. Lois turned in early."

"Alright. You two have a good night."

I finish my drink and walk out of the kitchen.

I'm passing my office to go up to bed when I hear something inside. I pause and listen at the door. It's quiet for a moment, but then I am sure I hear the sound of a drawer closing.

Without hesitation, I open the door to catch Mercedes sitting in my chair. She must have her nose in the bottom drawer because in her haste to come up, she hits her head on the still-open top drawer. She mutters a curse, rubbing the spot before fixing her face in a cool, indifferent expression.

I close the door behind me and set my briefcase on the floor. "Can I help you with something?"

She cocks her head to the side, takes a beat too long to answer. "I was looking for my phone."

"I gave you a phone."

"My old one. I have a number I need to get out of it."

"Whose number?"

"Just a number. Why do you have to know everything?"

"Because I'm not used to people snooping in my office."

"I'm not snooping. I'm looking for my own phone." She shoves the drawer closed, but it sticks, and she has to stand to use her hip to do it. I notice she's wearing a white camisole that comes to the very tops of her thighs. The peaks of her nipples press against the silk.

I produce a key out of my pocket, unlock the single-locked drawer, and take out her phone.

She tries to grab it, but I hold it out of reach. "It needs to charge. Let me know whose number you're looking for, and I'll get it to you tomorrow." I tuck the phone into my pocket.

"You were gone the whole day."

"I was. I thought you'd enjoy the time alone with your friends."

"It was a distraction. Don't think I don't know that."

"How was lunch?"

"Good. Did you find him?"

I raise my eyebrows.

She shakes her head. "And here I thought when you told me he was gone that you'd sent him away."

"My brother won't come near you again. I will see to that."

She folds her arms across her chest, inadvertently lifting her breasts and drawing my gaze to the soft swell of them. When she realizes what she's doing, she lowers them again.

"You shouldn't make promises you can't keep. I already told you that."

"I have no intention of breaking that promise. Now…"

I take her by the hips and tug her close, then turn her to face the desk. I press myself against her ass and brush her hair over her shoulder. She shudders when I run the scruff of my jaw over the beating pulse at her neck before sliding my chin along the curve of it as I bring my mouth to her ear.

"Put your hands on the desk, Mercedes."

She glances back, just barely, her breathing suddenly shorter as that pulse beats wildly. She sets her hands flat on the desk.

"Good girl." I take hold of her panties and drag them down over her thighs, letting them drop to her ankles before pushing her forward to bend her over the desk.

"What are you doing?" she asks breathlessly.

I put the toe of my shoe on the scrap of fabric around her ankles. "Step out." She does. I lift the camisole up to her waist and cup her ass with one hand, keeping the fistful of silk out of the way with the other. I spank her cheek lightly, testing.

She gasps and tenses. But otherwise, she doesn't move.

"Okay?" I ask.

She nods.

I do it again, harder this time, and release the silk to weave my fingers into her hair.

"What did you really want coming in here, little monster? Tell me or take your punishment." I spank, then rub the spot. I'm not worried about what she'd find in here. Anything important is locked up in a safe.

"Nothing."

I grin, then spank her ass once, twice. No rubbing this time.

She sucks in a breath, and I use her hair to tug her head backward.

"Try again," I tell her, slapping her legs apart and slipping my hand between them to find her wet sex. She moans when I rub her clit and whimpers when I spank it. "Mercedes?"

"I was just bored."

"Did you miss me?"

"No."

Smack. "Tell the truth."

"I didn't miss *you*. I missed your tongue." She turns her head a little and grins a sly grin. "I just wanted you to make me come again."

"There you go. That wasn't so hard, was it? You missed my tongue. All you have to do is say so."

She glances at the erection pressing against my slacks, then up at me.

"Get on your knees and make me come, Judge."

I raise my eyebrows, and it takes all I have not to laugh out loud at her command. Never before has a woman instructed me to kneel. Never will a woman order me to kneel.

"News flash, little monster. I eat you out

because I love the way you fucking taste. But I don't do it on your command." I smack her ass hard. "Stay. Understood?"

"Are you going to lick my pussy if I do as you say, Lawson?"

With a snarl, I release her and sit so I'm at eye level with her gorgeous ass. "Finger yourself."

Heat flushes her cheeks, but Mercedes is not one to back down so she does exactly as I know she will. She reaches between her legs and rubs her clit with a moan before pushing two fingers inside herself.

"Good girl. Very good girl." I unbuckle my belt and undo my slacks.

She licks her lips and moans for my benefit. "You like watching me fuck myself? Because you know I'll never let you fuck me again, right?"

"Careful or you'll eat your words, sweetheart."

"Are you going to jerk off watching me? Imagining my tiny little finger is your big, thick cock stretching my tight pussy?"

"You, my little monster, are a very dirty girl." I stroke myself over my briefs. "So dirty, I think you should take those wet little fingers of yours and smear them all over your asshole."

Her mouth falls open, eyebrows disappearing into her hair. The look is so comical I can't help my burst of laughter.

"Fuck you, you jerk!" She spins to face me as I

rise, her arm poised to slap me. I capture it, then the other, and secure both behind her back.

"It's cute when you get mad." My smile must so irritate her she actually snaps her teeth at me like she'd bite my face off if she could. "Makes me even harder for you."

"Let me go!"

She twists in my arms as I lift her onto the desk and kiss her lips, barely pulling back before she snaps again.

"I'd like to fuck your ass one day. I admit, I do imagine it when you have me jerking myself off twice a fucking day like I'm a goddamn teenager. Not yet, though. I don't think you're ready to take me in that tight little hole just yet."

She swallows hard, and it takes her a minute, but she does respond in true Mercedes fashion. "Like I said, Judge, you won't ever be fucking me again."

"No?" I tug her to me, grind against her, her pussy soaking my briefs before I push them down so there's nothing between us.

She looks down and sucks her lip between her teeth as I draw myself through her wet folds. She can't help her moan.

"You want to come, little monster?" I rub my dick up and down her pussy and push her backward, stretching her arms to opposite sides of the desk and pinning her by her wrists. "Tell me. Tell me you want to come, and I'll make you come. It's as easy as that."

"Your mouth," she says breathlessly, even as her legs open in invitation.

"I don't think my mouth will be enough tonight." Leaning over her, I swallow her moan when I kiss her. "I think you need something bigger inside you than my tongue."

"Fuck. I hate you!"

"But you want me all the same." I draw back a little, testing her with the head of my cock at her entrance. I watch her face, her eyes.

"Judge," she says.

"Lawson," I correct.

"Lawson," she breathes, and I push into her. "Oh. My. God."

"Fuck, Mercedes."

She is so slick and so tight I'm not going to last long. I intertwine my fingers with hers while moving inside, kissing her, not caring if she bites. Needing it too much.

She opens to me, taking my tongue in her mouth while my cock is in her pussy.

I shift my grip again, the fingers of one hand weaving into her hair, adjusting her hips with the other so I can get deeper inside her. She arches her back, her fingernails digging into my shoulders as she sucks on my tongue and comes so hard her throbbing walls milk me, and I almost don't pull out in time.

Because fuck. It's so fucking hard.

I want to come inside her so fucking bad that it takes all I have to finally pull out of her wet heat and trap my throbbing cock between us at the very last moment and come all over her.

8

MERCEDES

My experience may be pretty limited, but somehow, I don't believe the fire I have with Judge is something everyone has when it comes to sexual tension. When we come together, it's like fireworks. He lights the fuse, and I explode. But much like I suspected, just as soon as he's finished, he turns it off like a switch. His face returns to a neutral expression, and he dismisses me by telling me to go to bed.

I hate that about him. Even worse, I hate that I can't read him. There's no way for me to tell if he's dismissing me because he got what he wanted or he's trying to protect himself from feeling anything. I want to believe that might be the case, but I also don't want to be a fool.

My bed feels emptier without him, and I'm

not surprised when he doesn't join me. I don't expect to see him in the morning either, as it's typical for him to run off and put distance between us. So when he comes into my room with a scowl on his face, I arch an eyebrow at him in question.

"Can I help you?"

Irritation flickers across his features, and if I didn't know any better, it looks like I'm giving him a headache without even trying. That's about the time I notice he doesn't look rested at all. In fact, he looks fucking exhausted.

"Did you even sleep?" I ask.

Before he can answer the question, Lois and Miriam appear behind him and then shuffle into my room with boxes in hand.

"What's going on?" Dread trickles down my spine as they disappear into my closet.

"You're moving into my room," Judge grunts in answer.

"What?"

He doesn't look at all happy about this development, and it makes no sense.

"It's temporary," he assures me, but even he doesn't look convinced of that.

"I don't understand." My eyes move over his face. "Has something happened?"

He sighs and then checks his watch. "Get dressed. I'm taking you out for the day."

His avoidance of my question only irritates me more. "Is Santi okay?"

"Yes." His eyes soften at the concern in my voice.

"And Ivy?"

"The same," he says quietly.

I nod and get up, too tired to argue and not entirely sure I even want to know the reason behind the tension in his eyes. Things have only just begun to settle down, and I'm not certain I can handle anything else right now.

"Don't you have to work today?" I wander into my closet and start rifling through a section of dresses where Lois and Miriam aren't packing.

"I took the day off," Judge says from behind me. "Wear leggings."

I find it an odd request and wonder if it's a personal preference or if there's a reason behind it. But when I arch an eyebrow at him over my shoulder, all I receive in answer is a stony expression. The old me would have worn a dress just to be difficult, but I find that I don't feel like arguing with Judge today. So I grab a pair of leggings and an oversized tee shirt and go into the bathroom to change.

When I exit, he's waiting for me by the door to my bedroom, staring at what I know is my phone. By the renewed tension in his shoulders, I imagine he's seen something he doesn't like, but I can't think of what it might be. Other than the texts from Georgie, of course.

"Everything okay?" I ask, and he shoves it into his pocket, jerking his chin at me.

"Let's go."

As we climb into the Rolls Royce, it doesn't escape my notice that a guard from IVI sits in the front seat beside Raul. If that wasn't strange enough, another car waits behind us with three more.

Judge secures my seat belt for me absently even though I'm more than capable of doing it myself, and then we sit in stilted silence as Raul navigates us to wherever we're going.

"Judge."

He doesn't even seem to hear me, his gaze trapped outside the window, his mind clearly somewhere else.

"Judge." I touch his face, and he blinks. He looks at me, and something strange flickers through his eyes. Something that makes me nervous because he looks concerned.

"Is there anything else you need to tell me, Mercedes?" His voice is uncharacteristically quiet.

"What do you mean?"

"Are there any other unfinished schemes in your past I need to be aware of?" His eyes narrow slightly.

"No." My hand falls away. "Why?"

"Why were you in my office last night?" he demands. "What were you really looking for on your phone?"

Well, shit. I knew this question would come back to haunt me today, but I just didn't think it would be so head-on.

"I told you I was looking for a number." The big fat lie pours from my lips.

"What number?" His jaw clenches.

"A friend?" I don't mean for it to sound like a question, but dammit, it does.

"Whose name is...?" He waits, his eyes darkening.

"Ana," I blurt without thinking.

He doesn't say a word, and the conflict between us only gets thicker. I'm too proud to admit I was rifling through his office in search of evidence of his affection for another woman. Any other woman. I wanted to find something to bolster my campaign of not letting him back in. Something to fuel my ire and prove that he's a jerk of a liar just like me. But I found nothing. Not a single goddamned thing. And even though that doesn't mean he can be trusted, it means holding on to my anger is becoming increasingly difficult.

"Who the fuck is Ana?" he growls.

My eyes snap back to his, and I give him the pathetic excuse I hope won't rouse his suspicion.

"She's my aerial instructor. I just wanted to tell her I'm sorry I haven't been to class. That's all."

Judge doesn't quite look like he believes that, but something of an amused twitch curls his lip as the car comes to a stop unexpectedly.

"Funny you mention it." He nods to the familiar street outside. "You can tell her today."

My mouth falls open, and I stare at him in disbelief. "You're taking me... to class?"

He glances at his watch to hide his discomfort at the excitement in my voice. "You better hurry. You're going to be late."

"Okay, this is weird," Solana mumbles from her position on the silks beside me, eyeing the four guards standing on the street outside the studio before her gaze drifts back to Judge.

He's currently parked against the wall, his eyes on me as I shimmy farther up the aerial silk and then twist my body into an inverted bow pose. God, that feels good.

"Why does he look like he's about to have a heart attack?" Solana asks.

"Probably because he is." I smirk, flipping my body back upright and transitioning to splits.

Judge doesn't do well with situations he can't control, and it's obvious by the stiff expression on his face now, that's exactly what's happening. It hasn't escaped my attention that he's been inching closer and closer since class began, trying to appear a casual observer although he's clearly ready to spring into action at any moment should I slip.

For a minute, I amuse myself with thoughts of pretending to do just that, slipping down the silk and watching him jump to my rescue. But those thoughts are quickly doused with the reality he'd probably never let me come back to class again.

"The better question is who are those guys following you around?" Georgie asks from his position on the other side of me. "And will they come role play bodyguard with me?"

Solana and I both snort, and Georgie gracefully moves his body through the air, following the instructor's directions as we all transform to stag pose.

Unfortunately for me, it appears the gig is up when it comes to Georgie. Judge has started to piece it together since our arrival when he first noticed him in his spandex shorts and a tank top. But now, it's impossible not to notice Georgie has been practically drooling over the IVI guards with their ultra-serious expressions.

When I glance at Judge, his eyes move from Georgie to me, and I give him an amused smile. He shakes his head as if to let me know I'm going to pay for goading him unnecessarily later.

The rest of class passes quickly, far too quickly, and I'm disappointed when it's over. I had forgotten how good it felt to come here. To be with my friends and move my body this way. I'm hopeful Judge will let me do it again now that I seem to be earning some of his trust, but I'm also worried he only brought me here today as another distraction from whatever is really going on.

Solana seems to sense the shift in my mood, and she takes it upon herself to fix it, the way she has a habit of doing.

"Judge, you haven't seen my shop yet." She offers me a coy smile as she tosses her gym bag over her shoulder. "And I have it on good authority that we have one of the best coffee shops in the world right next door. The secret is chicory, of course."

Judge moves his gaze to me, and though I'm silent, he can see that I'm hopeful. I don't expect him to give in, honestly, but he does.

"I suppose we have some more time before we have to be home."

I sneak my hand over to his and give it a gentle squeeze of gratitude even though it seems somewhat ridiculous. I don't like requiring permission to do these things, but I'm used to it, and I'm also grateful that he's giving me more small freedoms.

We don't bother with the car when we exit onto the street. Instead, we walk the two blocks to Solana's shop on foot. It feels good to be back among these familiar places, but I can feel the strain radiating from Judge as he scans the street the entire time, checking for threats.

When Zen Apothecary comes into view, a familiar warmth spreads through my chest. Everything looks the same from the window. Inside, the quaint little shop has shelves made of reclaimed wood and old oak floors that creak when you step over them. Baskets of lavender and racks of potted plants adorn the entrance. It smells just as I remember it too. Incense, loose leaf teas, locally sourced herbal tinctures, essential oils, and Solana's line of skin care all combine to flood my senses. It's the scent of Solana. Of course, the aroma of coffee and beignets from next door doesn't hurt either.

"Take a seat." Solana gestures at the small bistro table in the corner. "I'll get the coffee called in."

Judge frowns, but before he can say anything, Madame Dubois enters the shop with a flourish, her long dress swishing around her feet. She's heading toward her small private corner of the shop where she resides during business hours as the in-house fortune teller. But before she can make it that far, she comes to a dead halt, her features pinching in distaste, and then she turns. At first, her eyes move over me, filled with obvious relief, and then they take on a hard edge as she turns to examine Judge.

"You." She points a steady finger at him as if she's cursing him. "Your fear does not serve you."

He arches an eyebrow at her, his face a mixture of amusement and annoyance. That is until she speaks again.

"Let go of the past before it robs you of what was always meant to be yours."

Something dark flashes through Judge's eyes, and even I find myself frowning. Madame Dubois has been known to be a little out there, and I always found her predictions to be more amusing than anything, but what she said seems to have struck a chord with Judge as he shifts in his chair uncomfortably.

"Someone's feeling feisty today," Georgie murmurs.

"You can say that again." I watch Madame Dubois take one more step before she pauses again and turns to me.

"It's good to see you back, but you should take care not to be so reckless."

And with that annoyingly accurate observation that Judge snorts at, she disappears behind her curtained area.

"Okay." Solana returns to us with a small paper bag in hand. "I think this should do it."

Judge stares at her in confusion as she hands it to him, and I smile at her. Even though she clearly thinks he's a beast, she can't help being herself.

"There's sandalwood incense and soap," she says. "And a mood elixir, well, for obvious reasons."

"Thanks," Judge grouses.

"Um, can you tell your guys to at least stand a little farther away from the shop door," she huffs as she stares outside. "They're scaring off all my patrons."

Judge looks like he's perfectly fine with the idea, and I don't doubt he's tempted to hand over his credit card and buy out the entire shop because right now, for whatever reason, he's still on edge. His eyes move over everyone that comes through the door, and he's checked my old phone twice since we've been here, which seems odd.

"What do you keep looking at on there?" I whisper as Georgie and Solana discuss the placement of her new air plant display.

"Nothing," Judge grunts in response.

Before there's any more time to argue, a guy wearing the familiar apron from the coffee shop next door enters. It's not the usual delivery boy who has a mad crush on Solana, so his eyes move over the shop before settling on Judge and me.

"Oh, here." Solana rushes over to greet him, taking the tray of coffees and the bag of beignets. "I was expecting Brady."

The guy nods, but his eyes don't move from Judge and me. "He's out sick today."

Solana frowns but shoves a few dollar bills into his hand for a tip and thanks him again. The guy lingers for another second, and I think he and Judge are having a silent pissing contest, which is weird, but then he disappears.

Solana sets the coffees down and opens the bag of pastries so we can all dig in. But before I can even reach for one, Judge glances at me.

"I don't think that's a good idea."

I stare at him in disbelief. Okay, whatever has him worked up is clearly making him overly paranoid.

"We order from them all the time," I assure him as I reach out and grab a pastry anyway. "Don't be so surly."

He tries to grab the pastry from my hand, and I taunt him with a smile as I shake my head and hold it up in the air. Georgie rolls his eyes.

"We've checked the ingredients exhaustively," he says dryly. "They are aware of Mercedes's allergy, and they don't use peanuts in any of their products."

Those words don't seem to pacify Judge, so I

gesture to my purse. "Don't worry, okay? I have my EpiPen if I ever need it, but I won't."

He doesn't look convinced, but there are some battles he's just going to have to get used to losing. I want my damned beignet, and I've eaten from this place a million times. It's not even an issue.

Before he can protest further, I stuff the doughy, sugary concoction into my mouth and take a bite. When I moan, Judge eyes me again like that annoys him too. Almost as if... dare I say it... that sound should be just for him.

Amusement makes me laugh, and powdered sugar falls from my fingers like snow as I nod to the bag. "Just try it. Then you'll understand."

He ignores my suggestion, and I can see he's just biding his time here, so I take the opportunity to take a couple more big bites and then follow it up with a drink of too-hot coffee. I'm sure he's going to insist we leave soon, and it makes me wonder what's next on our agenda. But as I'm considering it, something tickles my throat, and I cough a couple of times, trying to rid myself of the feeling. But it only intensifies, even as I drink more coffee and nearly choke on it.

"Mercedes?" Concern seeps into Judge's voice as he reaches for my face. "What is it?"

My blood pressure seems to plummet as I try to shake my head, assuring him it's nothing, but I know it's not. A wave of dizziness moves over me, and my throat feels tight. Too tight.

I reach for my purse, recognizing the symptoms of an allergic reaction I assured him I wouldn't have, and Judge curses.

"Oh, God," Georgie yelps at the same time Solana gasps. "Her face."

I'm not getting enough oxygen. That much is obvious to anyone.

"Here, let me do it." Solana tries to come around to help, but Judge seizes me and pulls me into his lap, tilting my head back.

"Get the goddamned EpiPen."

My vision is blurry with tears, but I can see Solana's trembling hand as she forks it over. "I can—"

Judge doesn't listen. He grabs the pen, jams it against my thigh, and tries to inject it. But I don't hear the telltale click, and he seems to be fighting with it as he digs it deeper, his voice betraying an edge of panic.

"Jesus Christ, what the fuck is wrong with this thing?"

"Let me try." I hear Georgie's voice fading like he's underwater.

They both start fidgeting with it and then comes the thing I really don't want to hear.

"There's something wrong with it," Georgie says. "This isn't right."

"Fuck!" Judge roars. "I'm calling the goddamned ambulance now."

He lays me on the shop's floor, and I try to look up at him, try to move to tell him it's okay, but I can't. I'm too sluggish. My throat feels like it's almost completely closed, and it's all I can do to focus on trying to drag in tiny gasps of air.

"I have another one!" Solana yells. "I have one here! It's behind the counter."

"Get it," Judge pleads. "Get it right now."

9

JUDGE

This is getting to be a bad habit. Mercedes passed out in my bed. Me watching her. Making sure she's breathing. Never wanting to witness another incident like the one in Solana's shop a few days ago.

I pick up her old phone again. Re-read the texts for the fucking hundredth time. Not that it makes any difference. I saw them when I switched it on after charging it to get her the number she claimed she was looking for when I caught her snooping. Pretty sure that was a lie anyway. It would be easy enough to get the number of her yoga instructor from either Solana or Georgie. The texts had been sent over the past several weeks, so for weeks, she's been in danger, and what the fuck have I done? Didn't even know about it.

She was a human being, you fucking cunt. You and your sort fucked her up. Now I'm going to fuck you up.

Cunt, you can't hide in your rich house with your rich boyfriend forever.

I'm coming for you, cunt. One way or another. I'm going to give you what you deserve.

They were all sent from different numbers, and Ezra's man hasn't been able to trace any of them. They couldn't pick up the slightest trail. Would Santiago be able to find something? I can't ask him. I can't tell him any of this. He has enough on his plate with the fates of Ivy and their unborn child unknown. I won't burden him with my failure to do the one thing he asked of me. Keep his sister safe.

I keep checking for a new text. Whoever sent these must know by now that he or she didn't succeed in the attack so I expect another one to be sent.

My phone vibrates with a call. I silenced it so as not to wake her. I pocket her phone and step out to answer when I see it's Ezra, leaving the bedroom door open a crack in case she needs me.

"Judge. How is Mercedes?"

"She'll be fine. She's sleeping." Thanks to the fact that Solana kept an EpiPen at the shop. She'd been doing it since she met Mercedes apparently. Georgie too.

"Good."

"What did you find?"

"Traces of peanut oil in the bag itself. They would have rubbed off on the pastries. The two in the bag were contaminated as well."

I try to remember the bag. Plain brown paper. I remember Solana commenting it wasn't the same kid who usually delivers to her.

"Anything on the man who delivered it?"

"The coffee shop's security was down for maintenance. The footage we grabbed from the shop across the street showed him intercept the kid who originally left with the order. The lens was dirty, the view fairly obstructed but we got lucky. There was a moment we had a clear shot and one of my guys was able to enhance the image enough. Between that and your description, I may have something for you."

"Go on."

"I'd prefer to confirm before I tell you."

"Just tell me. You can confirm after."

"Does the name Vincent Douglas ring any bells for you?"

My heart stops.

"Judge?"

"What did you say?"

"Douglas. Vincent Douglas."

No. It can't be.

"I'm guessing from that silence it does."

"Possibly." I clear my throat. "Does he have

family?"

"I haven't dug too deep. I was waiting on confirmation first."

"Dig. I need to know if he has family. A female relative. A wife maybe or a sister."

"I can do that. Shouldn't be hard to find."

I already know the answer. It's the only thing that makes sense. It's one of the things that had caught my attention when that man had walked into the shop. Something about him was strangely familiar. I hadn't been able to place it then but now, fuck. He'd looked at Mercedes and me with hate in his eyes. It had been so strange and out of place, but now it makes perfect sense.

The courtesan who had poisoned Santiago, whom Mercedes killed, I vaguely remember her from the Cat House from years ago. She'd always struck me as off. And the only reason I know her name is because of what Mercedes did. Because the name of that woman was Lana Douglas. And it would explain the threatening texts.

But Ezra Moore doesn't know anything about Lana Douglas's death. All he'll find is a missing woman.

"Judge? You still there?"

"Yeah, sorry. How is my brother?"

"Better. The doctor was right. He'd been injected with a cocktail containing enough fentanyl to kill a horse. He administered Narcan, which reversed the overdose. But Theron has a drug problem. You should think about what you want to do. He won't be able to walk away from this. He'll need professional help."

"Rehab?"

"Yes. I can take care of it if you need me to. I know a very good, very discreet facility."

"Where?"

"Just outside of Santa Barbara."

Santa Barbara. Good. Far enough away that I won't have to worry about him coming near Mercedes as I deal with this other mess. "Do it. Anything on the men who attacked him?"

"Still working on that."

"Jesus. What a fucking week."

"I'll let you know about Vincent Douglas as soon as I can."

"Thank you."

There's a pause. "Just one thing. Your brother is asking to see you."

"I'll think about it. Right now, my priority is Mercedes." At the mention of her name, I hear movement in the bedroom. I peer in through the open crack and see Mercedes is waking. "I'll talk to you later." I disconnect the call and reenter my bedroom.

"Good morning," I say.

She looks at the window. "Night, I think."

I follow her gaze and nod. "How are you

feeling?"

"Tired." She scratches her head, looking around.

"Headache? Anything? Do I need to have the doctor return?"

She shakes her head. "I'll be fine."

I sit on the edge of the bed and hand her the glass of water there. She takes a sip and hands it back. "Drink it all, will you?"

"I'm fine, Judge." She tries to get out of the bed, but I stop her and hold the water out. "Fine." She rolls her eyes but drinks, then hands the empty glass back to me.

"Have you had to use it before? The EpiPen?"

"When I was younger but I'm really careful." Her forehead creases, and I'm not sure if she's embarrassed or scared. I consider how much to tell her. "I eat beignets from there all the time. They know about my allergy."

"It happened. Just try to forget about it. Probably just an accident."

"The EpiPen in my purse didn't work, Judge."

I was hoping she wouldn't remember that part, but the EpiPen was tampered with. I wonder how long ago that had been done. I don't have to ask who did it. Miriam is missing. She left most of her things behind and took off. Her fingerprints were on the EpiPen although we all handled it, so it was kind of a mess. Ezra has men looking for her.

"I ordered more. I replaced the one in your bag. Put two in there in fact. Solana and Georgie have more as well. Just in case. I'll be keeping them in the cars and Lois has several in the kitchen. There will always be extra—"

"Judge," she says, stopping me. I watch as she pushes her hand through her hair, soft waves of it falling over her shoulders when she releases it. "Did someone tamper with it?"

"It was probably just faulty."

"Those things aren't faulty."

"Either way, you don't need to worry about that."

"Yeah, I kinda do."

I clench my jaw.

"You moved me in here before that happened. You've got security around me like I'm the Queen of England. What's going on?"

"Miriam is gone, Mercedes."

"Miriam?"

"I know what she did to you. The paperweight. I know you weren't lying, and I'm sorry I doubted you."

Her eyebrows rise, but it's not in an I-told-you-so way. More just in surprise. Probably from my apology. I think this is the first time I've apologized to her.

"I confronted her a little while ago," I tell her. It won't hurt her to know this.

"Why did she do it? I mean, she and I never really liked each other but fuck. She really hurt me."

I clear my throat. I'm not ready to tell her that part just yet. Because that secret would unravel far too many others.

"I don't know," I lie instead.

She studies me. "You think she messed with the EpiPen too?"

"I suspect so."

"But she's gone now. What does that mean exactly? Gone like Theron or…"

"I have men looking for her."

"Jesus, Judge! You knew what she did to me, and you didn't have her arrested or something?"

"There was more to it than that, and I was managing her. I felt it would be better to have her where I could keep an eye on her. That was clearly a mistake."

"That still doesn't answer my question. Why did you move me in here? Why the extra security?"

"With Abel having attacked Ivy like he did, I didn't want to take a chance he'd come after you, too." It is true. I have considered it. And I think this will be less frightening for Mercedes to deal with than knowing the brother of the woman she killed is out for revenge.

"Abel? He won't come after me. Why would he?"

"You're Santiago's sister. Not to mention you can testify against him to The Tribunal."

"Abel doesn't scare me."

Cupping her chin, I tilt her face up to mine. "Well, I'm not taking any chances with you. I will do what I need to do to keep you safe, little monster, even if I have to lock you away to do it."

"That was actually starting to sound sweet and then just got creepy."

I cup the base of her skull and pull her close. "I mean it, Mercedes. Seeing you like that the other day, feeling fucking powerless to fix it, it fucked with me."

"Be careful, Judge." She turns her huge eyes to me. She's so close that I see faint rings of gold inside them, and fuck, she's so beautiful, disarmingly so. "You don't want me to get the impression you care."

We look at each other for a long moment, and I know what she's waiting for. Confirmation. But nothing has changed between us. Nothing can change. I won't marry her. I can't. And she's right. I can't give her false hope.

So I change the subject. "Georgie's gay."

She searches my eyes, and I see her disappointment, but then she grins. "It took you a really long time to figure that out."

"Why did you let me believe you two were together?"

"I didn't. You believed that all on your own."

"You certainly didn't correct me. And those texts. Any man would believe what I believed."

"Haven't you ever just had a really easy, fun friendship? Someone you don't have to be all intense Judge-like with?" That last part she says with a mock-serious tone.

I don't know why I'm taken aback by this. Almost confused. My friendships are serious. They always have been. I've never had a relationship with anyone like what I have seen between Mercedes and her friends.

"Oh, my God, you haven't. That's actually kind of sad, Judge," she says without a note of mockery.

Before I can reply, my phone vibrates. "I need to take this." I get up, grateful for the interruption.

I unlock the phone and read the text. *One sister. Lana Douglas. Whereabouts unknown.*

Fuck.

"What is it?"

"Nothing. Are you hungry?"

"You keep so many secrets."

"Says the woman with a second life. Hungry?"

"You're going to tell me what the hell is going on."

"Nothing's going on. Come on," I draw the blanket away and hold out my hand. "Get dressed. We'll have dinner downstairs."

10

JUDGE

I pay my mother a visit early the following evening. She greets me in the kitchen, pouring herself a large glass of wine.

"Well, look who bothered to drop by," she says, her back to me. "You going to call your dog off now?" She's essentially been under house arrest since Miriam disappeared and before that, since the incident with Theron, I'd been having her followed.

"Evening, mother." I sit down without waiting for an invitation because I'm not going to get one.

She turns to me, leans against the counter with her glass in her hands. "Are you here to tell me you've heard from my son?"

Her disdain of me, her very clear preference for Theron even after all he's done shouldn't bother me, but it still stings.

"Theron will be spending time in a rehab facility. Did you know about his addiction?"

"He's not addicted. He just enjoys life."

"Jesus. Are you so fucking blind?"

"He's had a hard time of it, Judge. Not that you'd know about that."

"I know plenty."

"Which facility? I'll go see him."

"I don't think so. Sit."

She raises her eyebrows.

I push the chair out with my foot. "Sit. Now."

She raises her chin. "You sound exactly like him, you know that?"

My grandfather. I don't bother to comment. She's goading me. Instead, I wait until she's parked herself in the seat.

"You realize I can take everything away from you, don't you?"

"Like you did your brother?"

"My brother hurt someone."

"Not just anyone." She smirks, sips her coffee. "I know you're used to getting your way but you're wrong on this one. That woman used him and got what she deserved."

"He beat her."

"A sex game that got out of hand."

It takes all I have not to leap across the table and shake some sense into her. "I'm not here to discuss Theron. I'm here to talk about Miriam."

"Miriam? Why would you need to talk about Miriam with me? She's the help." So cold. And said without the slightest change to either tone or expression. My mother is an accomplished liar. But she's also dangerous because according to Miriam, she knows Mercedes's secret.

"I know who she is," I say.

"I don't know what you're talking about."

"Theron's father's sister. Which makes her his aunt. Family, really, to Theron at least. And I know what you and she planned, putting Mercedes in Theron's path—"

"What's this about, Judge? Are you going to haul your own mother into court for trying to play matchmaker?"

"I wasn't finished."

"Well, heaven forbid anyone interrupt you, your honor."

"I want to know if you had anything to do with the attack on Mercedes a few days ago."

"What attack? What kind of person do you think I am exactly?"

"You know she has a peanut allergy. Miriam would have told you that. Her fingerprints were on the EpiPen that was tampered with." Her face loses a little color. "The beignets that caused the allergic reaction—"

"Wait a minute." She drinks a big swallow of wine and I wonder how many she's had. The bottle is nearly empty. "So your girlfriend ate some beignets that made her sick and you're trying to blame me for that?"

I ignore the girlfriend part and stand. "She could have died. Do you understand that?"

"Died? Judge... You're exaggerating, I'm sure."

"I can assure you I'm not."

"I didn't have anything to do with any tampering. If Miriam did something—"

"Vincent Douglas, mother. Vincent Douglas delivered the beignets to her."

She looks at me blankly.

"Do you know where he is?"

"I don't even know who he is much less where."

"He will try to hurt her again."

"This has nothing to do with me. I don't know who that is. Why would I?"

I stop short of mentioning the courtesan because what if Miriam was lying about having told her? What if she doesn't know? I can't be the one to tell her. Give her more ammunition.

"Look, yes I knew who Miriam was when I had your grandfather hire her. She was down on her luck and considering the situation, why not help her out. God knows I didn't have any other allies in this house. But the peanut thing, she may have mentioned your girlfriend's allergy but I swear I didn't know it was lethal. I just thought her face would swell up or something. What do I know about these things? If Miriam fed her peanuts, that's on her, not me. Probably a stupid little game she concocted. Miriam doesn't like Mercedes either. Seeing a pattern?"

I snort.

"What you're saying now, though? That it was some sort of attack? That has nothing to do with me, Judge. Why would I care about that woman? I don't like her, it's true. But I don't like any of those high-born spoiled Society women. They look down their noses at me and I've never made a secret of my dislike. You know that. But I can tell you I don't care enough to launch some attack. Christ. Not everyone thinks like your grandfather. If anything, you're blood, not me. Maybe question your own motives with her. Do you have any intention to marry her? Because if you don't, I suggest you try to keep yourself to yourself. A woman like that will trap you. You don't want that."

"You're concerned for me?"

"Of course, I am. You're my son."

"Or is it that if I marry and have an heir, it won't bode well for Theron, especially considering what he did to her."

"Like I said, a sex game."

I slam my hands on the table so hard she jumps. "If you fucking say that one more time, I swear—"

"What?" she stands. "You'll take me into that

room and finish what your grandfather started? Oh, believe me, I have no doubt you would."

Jesus.

I walk away, rub the back of my neck. She got a rise out of me. I just gave her exactly what she wanted.

"Does your girlfriend know about that by the way? Or about your temper? Just like his. It's a matter of time. She should really know what she's in for, don't you think? I doubt she'd so easily spread her legs—"

I spin to face her and throw the table over, sending wine all over the kitchen, red splashing on her white robe before the glass shatters into a hundred pieces.

My mother screams.

I stand staring at her, at the splatters of red so much like blood.

She's backed against the counter and staring back at me. She steels herself. Is she truly terrified of me? "I feel sorry for the woman you'll marry one day. You are just like him, Judge. Exactly him."

I flinch as if she's struck me and stalk out of the cottage, her accusations chasing me. Nothing I haven't heard before, I remind myself. Nothing I don't already know. I am like him. I will hurt her. It's in my nature.

I stalk to the one place I know I should avoid. I walk over muddy earth, my boots sinking into the ground. He'd hate that. Me tracking mud inside. I don't use my flashlight to light the way as I retrieve the key from my pocket and unlock the padlock, push the door open. Feeling for the switch I flip it and light up the room. I'm instantly confronted by the evidence of my brother's rage. His hate. The whip on the floor. The broken cane. Mercedes's shoes discarded, one in a corner, the other upside down a few feet away. Her clothes, torn from her body. If I look close at the whipping bench, I see blood too. Hers?

At the fireplace I stack wood. Using old paper for kindling I light it and it takes immediately. The logs are so dry they'll go up in no time. Satisfied, I straighten, watch the fire grow, flames bright and hot.

I take the bottle of scotch I drank from the last time I was here and carry it to his chair. No one sat in that damned chair but him. Ever. It's huge, like a fucking throne, the leather creased and worn. I switch on the CD player, my grandfather never understood streaming, and Matthäeus Passion blares at a volume that at first makes me flinch. I drink straight from the crystal decanter.

This is what he'd listen to after the punishments. While we lay limp trying not to make a sound. Like what he'd done was some sort of holy rite. During the punishments there was silence. Mostly. Because it was a game to him. How long until we'd scream. And woe to he who wept. Tears are weakness. Screams are also weakness but somehow less so. Take it like a man, he'd say. And until you did, he kept going. Never tiring. Taking a sick pleasure from it.

I spent some time over that bench but not nearly as much as my own father, even as an adult man. Never as much time as Theron. He was always finding some way to make trouble. Like he didn't learn. Or maybe he just wanted grandfather's attention desperately enough that he didn't care if it was good or bad.

As far as I know my mother was only brought here that one time. But maybe I'm wrong. I know he taunted my father about his inability to control his wife. I think my grandfather hated her. Once she served her purpose, bearing his grandsons, he didn't bother with her. Until he learned the truth about Theron. Then she had his full, undivided attention. And I was made to witness.

Jesus.

Can I blame her for hating me?

I push my hand through my hair roughly, drink three long swallows of scotch, then three more until I start to feel it. The heat. The numbing will come. But not fast enough so I drink more.

My mother is right. I will hurt Mercedes.

Because my grandfather favored me for a reason. He chose me over my father, over Theron even before he knew Theron wasn't blood. It wasn't because I was the firstborn. It was because he saw something in me he liked. He saw himself. His sharpness of mind. His disciplined nature. His need for balance between right and wrong, justice and consequence.

And he saw his own rage.

I would carry the family after his death. It had been decreed from when I was only sixteen. My father had accepted it. He'd had no choice once my grandfather learned the truth about Theron's true paternity. Ironically, it was my father who had given him that piece of information. I still don't understand why he did that. Was he so afraid of my grandfather? Was he so controlled by him that he would deliver his wife to the old man? That he would ensure the destruction of Theron's future? Or did he do it to punish my mother for humiliating him with her affair?

The music reaches its crescendo as I finish the bottle. I get to my feet and I hurl the decanter against the far wall. The sound of expensive crystal smashing is momentarily satisfying. It feels good. Violence feels good. It always has if I'm honest with myself.

I stalk toward that wall, glass crunching under my shoes as I tear the racks that hang there down. The music drowns out my thoughts while I rip the room apart, instruments of torture, some for show, some for use. I don't discriminate. I destroy them all, tearing down shelves, turning over benches, ripping leather from wood.

His books I tear in two before feeding them to the fire. I open the cigar box. Still half a dozen in here. I pick one up, smell it. Nothing quite takes me to that dark time as this smell. It still lingers in my study too. I should tear the walls down. Throw away anything the stench clings to no matter its value. I should bury any memory of him, including his portrait, and maybe with it I can bury this side of myself.

But as I look around the room, at the destruction I caused, I know I can't. I know that's not a possibility.

I drop the box to the floor and open the cabinet where more bottles of scotch are lined up in a neat row. I take one, twist the cork and break the seal to drink from it, feeling the burn on its way down. I'm about to start on the second part of the room when I hear a noise. Barking. The dogs.

I turn to the door. And standing there in black leggings and my Barbour that's entirely too big on her is Mercedes, her hair loose and soaked down her back. Her riding boots caked with mud. I wonder if she, too, walked. The dogs stop at her side as if she were their master and not I and they all watch me, the dogs curious, Mercedes something else as she takes in the state of things. The state of me.

"Kentucky Lightning came back without you." She enters the room. "What the hell are you doing, Judge?"

I don't know why I feel so caught out. Like she's seeing some part of me she was never meant to see. A part that I've worked very hard to hide.

"You don't answer your fucking phone and it's pouring out so the dogs can't pick up your scent. Your mother said you left over an hour ago in a rage. What did you do to her? She looked terrified. What the fuck is going on?"

Paolo comes running into the room stopping short when he sees me. "You were right," he says to Mercedes.

"Take the dogs back," Mercedes tells him without taking her eyes off me. "I'll stay with him."

Paolo looks unconvinced especially when his eyes dip to the bottle. "I don't think that's a good idea."

She turns to Paolo. "I'm fine. Go."

"No, he's right, Mercedes. You need to go," I say.

She makes a point of sweeping her gaze over the room. "I don't think so. Unless you're coming with me."

"Paolo," I say.

Paolo takes her arm but she shrugs it off. She turns to him. "Go. I'll be fine."

Paolo looks between us.

"I'll be fine," she repeats.

He gives me one last glance then nods, and leaves with the dogs. Mercedes closes the door. She goes to the CD player and turns the music off. The sudden silence is heavy, like a solid thing.

I watch as she strips off my coat and drops it on the leather chair. Grandfather would have had a fit.

She comes right up to me and takes the bottle from my hand. Never taking her eyes from me she drinks a long swallow.

"You should have gone with Paolo."

"Why? Because you're drunk?"

I reclaim the bottle and drink, then set it aside. "Go to the house. Now."

She cocks her head to the side and steps closer. "No."

"I don't want to hurt you."

"You won't."

"You don't know that. Don't know me."

"Then show me. Show me just how big and bad you are, Lawson Montgomery."

11

MERCEDES

Judge stares down at me, eyes alight with torment. There's a war inside his head, and right now, I don't know which side is winning.

"Why would you come back here?" he demands.

I study the lines of his face, and I realize there's always been something tormented in him. He hides it well, but it's there, beneath the surface. Beneath the tension that creeps in around his eyes whenever someone tries to get too close, just as I'm doing now.

"I learned a long time ago not to let the places where bad things happen have power over me." I reach out to smooth the shirt collar around his neck. "If I did, I'd never be able to go anywhere, and that includes half of your property since I've been in your care."

He flinches at the observation, but there's no point in sugar-coating it. We both know the truth.

"It's the world we live in." I lean into him, feeling the warmth of his chest as it presses against my body. "There's no point denying it. This is our normal."

"It doesn't have to be." He shakes his head, a dark expression taking over him. "Not for you, Mercedes."

"Why?" I trail my fingers up the length of his neck, stroking his jaw. "Because you're going to give me away? You think I'll be better off with someone else?"

His jaw clenches, and he tries to brush my hand away, but I resist and then he captures it between us.

"Yes," he grits out. "It's something you will come to understand in time."

His determination stings, but that's nothing new.

"And what happens when my husband turns out to be a monster too?" I trap him with my eyes. "When he decides I need to be beaten and whipped for my own good, will you still think I'm better off then?"

"I would never let that happen," he snarls.

"But you'd have no choice." I give him a pained

smile. "It's a man's business what he does at home with his wife. At least in our world. You wouldn't be able to rescue me, Judge. Not anymore. I've always known it would be up to me to rescue myself."

"Mercedes." His words are thick with restraint. "I know what you're doing."

"What am I doing?" I ask innocently as I yank my hand from his and resume my exploration of his skin.

"You're goading me."

"Am I?" I cock my head to the side. "I don't see it that way. I'm telling you a truth. You want to give me away, and—"

"I can't fucking marry you!" he roars.

The ferocity in his tone makes me freeze, and when I recover from the flinch and dare a glance up at him, I know this is the beast inside him coming out to play.

"I know you won't." I force the words up my raw throat. "You said you'd never marry at all. Tell me why, and then we'll never discuss it again."

He drags himself away from me, taking another long pull from his scotch. I haven't ever seen Judge drink this much, and admittedly, it's a little disturbing. But I know this might be the only time I get my answers from him.

"Because Theron was right." His eyes are inky pools of black when he turns his gaze back on me.

"You don't understand the things I'm capable of. The darkness that lived in my grandfather lives in me too. I can only keep it caged for so long before it's inevitable I end up hurting someone."

"That's not who you are," I argue.

"It is." He hurls the bottle of scotch at the wall, and it shatters, making me wince.

"We all have a monster inside us." I rush to get the words out as the vein in his neck pulses, his anger rising. "But we have free will too. It's up to you to decide—"

"You don't know what he did." His words echo off the walls, ricocheting around us like shrapnel. "To my mother. To my grandmother. They were subservient to his monster, and any wife of mine would be too. It's the path I'm destined for."

"Bullshit!" I hurl the words back at him, my voice choking desperately as he stalks toward me in a fury. "That's not who you are. It's just the lie you tell yourself."

"Shall we test that theory?" He cages me in against the stone wall with his arms, his breathing ragged, his voice unrecognizable.

"Threaten me all you want." I bring a trembling hand to his chest, settling it over his beating heart. "I know what's in here. I've seen it."

"God, you really are delusional." He laughs mockingly.

"Fuck you." I shove him hard to provoke him.

"You want to be an asshole, then do it. Hurt me. Give it your best shot. But I should warn you, you better come prepared to top the great Lorenzo De La Rosa. Unless you carve scars as deep as his in my flesh, then I'll see you as nothing more than weak."

Judge's nostrils flare, and he seizes my wrist, yanking me so close his breath feels like fire against my lips. "Do. Not. Fucking. Test. Me."

"Oh, but I want to." I lean up on my toes, snaring his lip between my teeth before I bite and taste the copper of his blood. "Come out and play, beast. Show me your worst."

He drops my hand, his palm whipping toward me to wrap around my throat, collaring me. "Is this what you want?" He rumbles in my ear, his voice a mixture of sensual and sinister.

"Yes," I wheeze. "Fuck me like you fuck your courtesans. Show me what you like."

A low growl reverberates from his throat as his eyes flash. "That's what you want?"

"Yes," I say, less certain this time.

"Careful what you wish for." He drags a thumb over my lips in what feels like a possessive way, but then all too soon, his demons summon him back to them. "Take off your clothes and get on your fucking knees."

There's a moment of hesitation on my part, and he sees it. He relishes it. Because he wants to win.

He wants to scare me and prove his point. I want to challenge him and prove mine. But only one of us is drunk right now, and there's an uncertainty in me about how far each of us will go to win the war.

Still, I started this battle, and I refuse to back down. So with trembling fingers, I pull off my clothes and toss them onto the overturned table. Judge stares at me, cold and appraising before he steps forward. Without warning, he slaps my breast hard, and I hold back a yelp.

"I told you to get on your fucking knees."

Biting back the retort on my tongue, I force myself to remember this is a game. And I'm determined it's a game he's going to lose.

I lower myself to my knees, the cold stone rough against my flesh. Judge circles around me, stroking my hair and then my face. Against my will, my eyes seem to flutter shut, soaking up that moment of affection that's so rare from him. But all too soon, he snatches it away with a harsh command.

"Is this how you greet a Sovereign Son?"

His unspoken request rattles me. I know what he wants. What he expects. This is our world, and even if I am a Society daughter, he will always rank higher. Always be more. It takes everything inside me to bow forward in the way I was taught. I've never done this for anyone, but I've seen it done at weddings. I've seen the way wives kneel at their husband's feet, showing their respect to the gods who walk among us.

"Dominus et Deus," I whisper.

Judge's gaze burns into the top of my head, and I know by the long silence, he's not going to let me half-ass this.

"Is that all the respect you have to give me?"

"No." I lower my head further, doing the one thing I swore I never would. I kiss his shoe and then the other, silently at war with myself.

When his fingers caress the nape of my neck, it soothes some of the sting, and I realize something I could never confess out loud. He's the only man I would ever do this for. He's the only man I'd even consider worthy of my submission. And I wonder if he's thinking about it too. I wonder if he's imagining me doing the same before someone else, and if it bothers him.

"Does it please you?" I ask him softly.

Silence is my response.

"Do you think it will please my husband too?"

"I think you have a long way to go in learning how to please a man," he answers coldly. "But you can start by sucking my cock."

The ice in his words wounds me as I'm sure he intended, but I don't let him see it as I raise my head and reach for his zipper.

"I must not be too displeasing," I murmur haughtily as I unwrap his throbbing erection like a

Christmas gift. "Or are your standards just that low?"

"I'm a man," he utters in a strained voice. "Any hole will do."

Again, it feels like a slap in the face, but I know that's his intent. So I decide to play along and act like one of his women from the Cat House.

"Lucky for you, I have three of them."

His eyes blaze, and I feel a little too smug as I drag him into my mouth and flick my tongue against the salty head of his cock. He's big, and it's hard for me to fit him, but I try to take as much as I can, hoping for some sign of a reaction. But he gives me absolutely nothing.

"Is that the best you've got?" he asks with a bored tone.

It fucking irritates me, so I drag him deeper into my mouth, sucking harder, and even though I feel his dick pulsing against me, he gives me no other reaction.

"Remind me why we're doing this," he says. "Because I'm starting to feel like I'm not getting my money's worth. Do you want a real whore to teach you how it's done?"

I pause and glare up at him, and he meets my gaze with an empty expression.

"Carlisle always said if you want something done right, you have to do it yourself." He sighs and grabs a handful of my hair, and then thrusts his cock so deep I nearly choke.

My hands fall against his thighs, holding him as he does it again.

"That's more like it," he breathes, tipping his head back so I can't see his face. "Now you understand. This is what you're here for."

"Fuck you," I mumble around him.

He chokes out a bitter laugh and thrusts his hips forward, making me gag. Any decency I was trying to hold on to goes out the window as spit drips down my chin. My eyes water, and I can feel the mascara running rivers down my face. But I don't protest. Instead, I wrap my arms around him and stroke his muscular ass, encouraging more.

Despite his best efforts, a groan catches in his throat, and he thrusts into my mouth again, punishing me for it. And then we fall into a rhythm. Him using my face like a fuck toy, me humming my approval against him.

If I'm honest, I'm not even faking it. Because something is insanely hot about Judge like this. Dominating me. Taking what he wants from me. A terrifying part of me thinks I'd probably give him anything he wants. It's something I can't breathe life into. At least, not when we're done playing this game. He reminds me of that a second later when he thrusts, gags me, and then pulls his wet dick free from my mouth.

"This display is a little pathetic," he growls. "Don't you think?"

"What?" I blink up at him, confused.

"You aren't supposed to enjoy it."

"What if I do?" I study him.

"Then maybe you really are a whore." He pulls me by the hair until I fall forward, my hands catching against the stone. "But you're still not half as good as my best."

Those words cut me deep. Too deep. And it has the immediate effect of dousing me in cold and robbing any of the pleasure I felt from this twisted scenario. But it only gets worse when he shoves my face down onto the floor, rubbing it in the dirt.

"There's nothing special about you." He positions himself behind me, sliding his cock against me before he thrusts into me so hard that I jolt. "You're just a body with three holes, exactly like you said. At least the other women actually try."

His verbal tirade doesn't end there, and I know now I was a fool to think I could ever win against a man like him. Judge proves it with every scathing insult he tosses my way.

"I took you because I was bored." Thrust. "Because you were easy." Thrust. "It means nothing to me." Thrust. "It never will."

Despite all my bravado, tears leak from my eyes and splash into the floor beneath me. I don't want him to see, and I can't feel anything anymore as he pounds into me, using me exactly the way I asked him to. Why couldn't I see how dangerous this was? Why couldn't I believe him when he warned me?

"Tell me how much you like it now," he snarls.

A choked sob bursts from my lips before I can stop it, and Judge freezes behind me, his hands digging into my hips. But when he reaches down and tries to move my hair away, tries to see the vulnerability on my face, I can't handle it.

"No." I sever our connection, crawling away from him and stumbling to my feet before I break into a run.

I know it's stupid. I'm fucking naked. Covered in spit and dirt and shame. But I run from the building, into the darkness, only to be snatched from behind and dragged back inside.

"No!" I scream. "Let me go!"

"Mercedes." His voice has a raw edge that wasn't there a minute ago. But I refuse to believe he has any feelings now. I can't.

"Mercedes." He drags me against him, hauling me back to the room of torture, and collapses into the chair, holding me hostage against his chest.

"Look at me," he commands.

I don't.

"Give me those dark eyes. Let me see you." His voice is softer now, more pleading and less... whatever it was five minutes ago.

"No." I bury my face into his chest, using my hair as a shield, but it doesn't protect me.

He drags it away, unveiling me, grabbing me by the chin and forcing my gaze to his.

"You said it's what you wanted." Annoyance and shame color his tone.

"I was wrong." The words heave from my chest. "You win, Judge. You fucking win."

There's a long moment of silence, and I use it to gather my strength.

"Tell me it was a lie, or let me walk away forever. Let me go."

His arms tighten around me, and he shakes his head. "I'm not letting you go."

"I won't stay." My voice wavers, but there's no doubt I mean it. "I will fight and claw every day until I get out of here. Even if I have to kill myself to do it."

"No." The word lashes from his tongue so violently that I can't deny he means it too. "You aren't leaving me."

"Why do you care?" I rasp. "I'm nothing. You said so yourself."

"You aren't nothing." He's shaking when he brushes his fingers over my face with more affection in one touch than I've ever had in my whole life. "You already know that. It's why you wanted to play this stupid fucking game in the first place."

"I don't know that." My eyes close so I can't

look into his, get lost in them. "What you said felt real. Too real."

"How does this feel?" He cups the back of my head and kisses me, melting some of my resolve. "How does it feel every time you steal a piece of my soul like the little thief you are?"

Another kiss. I don't kiss him back, but I can feel the tension dissolving between us, regardless of how hard I try to cling to it.

"How does it feel to know nobody else has ever had my kiss?" he asks, his fingers digging into me.

When I open my eyes to meet his, the shock of his words tugs at something deep inside me.

"Is that true?"

"What do you think?" He grabs my ass and yanks me closer, making me straddle him. "I've broken every goddamned rule with you."

"Except the one that matters most," I whisper.

His answer is to kiss me again, and maybe I shouldn't let him off so easy, but I do. I think Judge has given me more truths in the last two minutes than he's ever given anyone. And right now, there's a burning ache deep inside me only he can satiate.

"Show me," I murmur against his lips, my hands moving over the broad expanse of his chest. "Show me what you really want."

A growl vibrates from his lips into mine as he lifts my body and slides me down his cock, settling me on top of him. My fingers find their home in his hair, and he gives me something new, something different. It's no less intense, but it's softer, the way his lips move over my jaw and down my throat, sucking at the sensitive skin there.

"I took you because I couldn't help myself." The confession spills free on a ragged breath. "Because you are so goddamn addictive, you've fucking cursed me the way you curse all men, little monster."

I whine against him as his palms settle on my ass, pivoting my hips so I'm rocking down over his thick cock, splitting me open in more ways than one.

"There's no comparison." He drags his nose down my neck, inhaling me. "You've eclipsed everyone else. Blinded me to their faces, their memories. Is that what you want to hear?"

I bite back a whimper and nod. "If that's the truth."

"It is," he answers roughly. "Goddammit, Mercedes, how can you not see it?"

Another tear leaks from my eye, and he leans up to kiss it away. At that moment, the last of my resistance fades away, and I fall into him, squeezing his face in my palms. I kiss him, and he grunts at its savagery, returning it with equal passion by fucking me like it's his last day on earth.

Somewhere between us are the words we can't bring ourselves to say. I'm trapped, and so is he.

We both know it. We're drowning in it. Drunk on it. Desperate for another fix. These feelings are too tangible to ignore, and the more we give in, the more I'm aware that we feed off each other. And I fear that only one of us will be strong enough to walk away in the end. I know when I shatter around him and look into his eyes, it won't be me.

I also know when Judge tips his head back, groaning as he comes inside me, he isn't just going to break me. He's going to destroy me.

12

MERCEDES

Judge looks up at me with a sleepy, sexy softness as he pins my hips in place, grunting as water sloshes over the edges of the bathtub, and he comes inside me. Again. He stays there, his warmth flooding my body, soaking into me like he's branded me in a way nobody else ever can.

I can tell by the lack of concern he's not thinking about the consequences right now. I don't know if he'll even remember it tomorrow. He's been fucking me for three hours, and even still, he can't seem to keep his hands off me.

His head falls back against the tub with a thud, but his hands continue their leisurely exploration of my body, stroking over my ribs, my breasts, all the way up to the back of my neck. The area he touches often in moments like these. Without a doubt, I know if he were to ask for it right now, I would give that space to him. But I know better than to believe in things like that.

Tonight, we're in a dream-like haze. Tomorrow, when Judge wakes, he'll go back to what he knows. The walls he's built will resurrect themselves, the shutters will come down, and I'll be fighting to gain so much as an inch back into this space we're in now.

Maybe it's not fair play, but I decide I may as well grasp the opportunity while I have it. He's pliable. He's open. And I want to know what has kept him so guarded all these years.

"Tell me about your mother," I whisper against his lips.

He sighs, eyelids falling shut as he mumbles his response. "What's there to tell? She hates me."

The admission surprises me because I didn't sense that at all. I mean, it was obvious his mother wasn't winning any awards for affection. But she seemed much like any other vapid Society matron during my brief interactions with her. Sure, she was fake, but most of them are. I just assumed it was with me, not Judge.

"Why?" I press. "Why would she hate you?"

"Because I didn't protect her," he answers quietly. "I let Carlisle beat her for her indiscretion, and I didn't say a goddamned word to save her."

His admission sucks the air from my lungs, but

I can't let him know it. He's talking, and I'm aware there's only a brief window of time before he'll stop and shut this door forever.

"Why?"

"You said it yourself." He blinks open his unfocused eyes. "This is the world we live in. I was sixteen, and Carlisle's word was law. She's never forgiven me for it, and she never will."

The truth splits my heart in half. Because as much as I pity his mother for what she must have endured at the hands of his grandfather, my heart aches for Judge too. I understand better than anyone what it's like to be trapped in an impossible situation. I learned that from watching my brothers trying to sacrifice themselves to save me. It never worked. They would take beatings, but I would too. It didn't stop my father, and I know it wouldn't have stopped Carlisle either.

"And what about this?" My fingers move to the tattoo wrapping around his back, over the scar he's tried to hide. "What happened here, Judge?"

His eyes snap to mine, and suddenly, he looks stone-cold sober, and I know the time for answers is over.

"Let that be a lesson to you." He pulls his cock from me and hoists me up, splashing water everywhere as he helps me from the tub. "That's what happens when you trust someone. There's no such thing as loyalty, little monster. We all have to learn the hard way."

13

JUDGE

As I sip my coffee, I scroll through Mercedes's old phone, looking for any clues I missed. Anything at all. No new threats have come in. It's quieter than I expect, which is worrisome.

Vincent Douglas knows by now that Mercedes survived his attack. So why hasn't he sent another message? Another threat?

According to Ezra, Douglas is a steelworker at a company in Baton Rouge. He's quiet, keeps to himself, and they've never had trouble with him. He shows up for work, does his job, and goes home.

A few weeks ago, though, Douglas quit without notice and simply disappeared. I've had men at his apartment, a small, basic accommodation. Cleaner than I expected. He had paid rent for the following month, according to the landlord. For a small fee, however, he was willing to let us into Douglas's apartment where his things still were, including photos of himself with his sister. A lot of photos. They were close. Further investigation into Lana's life proved that. They grew up together in foster care. Close enough in age, they managed to stay together until Lana turned fifteen and Vincent sixteen.

That's where there's a hole in Vincent's history. A sealed record. One I was able to access given my position. And the story is one I've heard too often. Trouble with a foster parent for Lana. Vincent got involved. He was getting to be a big guy by then. The parent was beaten badly, and both Vincent and Lana were removed from the home. Vincent spent the next two years in juvenile detention while Lana went to another home.

Once he was out of juvie, she ran away, and I imagine they lived together. She was almost eighteen by then. There are blips of their lives over the next few years. Working odd jobs to get by. Neither of them had friends. And then Lana came to work at the Cat House, and Vincent stayed in Baton Rouge. One letter that had been ripped apart and then taped back together tells of their deteriorating relationship. His disapproval of her choice of profession. Her apologies. That was more recent than I liked, and I have a feeling he came to see her and found her apartment empty. It would have been cleaned by then. And somehow, he's figured out what happened to her. And Mercedes's role in it. Although he can't know for certain. But that won't matter to someone like him. This man is not a man to reason with. He's become violent when protecting his sister before. And I don't believe, for a second, he'll walk away from this.

Men with nothing to lose are the most dangerous of all. And I get the feeling Vincent Douglas has nothing to lose.

"Sir?" Raul enters the dining room, where I'm drinking coffee as I wait for Mercedes to come down after her shower. "I have what you needed."

He hands me a plain brown paper bag.

"Thank you, Raul."

"No problem, sir."

I pocket the phone, set my coffee aside, pour a mug for Mercedes, and head upstairs to my bedroom. The shower is still going when I enter, so I sit on the bed to wait. The door is open, but it's so steamy she doesn't see me as I watch her silhouette.

I need to be careful with her now. I've already gone too far. I had when I touched her at all because even in those first days, she was different from any other. I knew it all along. Maybe before I even took custody of her.

But what happened in the punishment room?

And in the hours following? That was just fucking irresponsible if not outright stupid. She's not on birth control, and I should know better. But the image of her on her knees before me, my cock stuffed down her throat as mascara ruined her perfect face? Fuck. It's burned itself into my memory, and I'm hard at the thought.

The water switches off, and I blink out of my reverie. I get up to grab a towel. She is momentarily surprised to see me, then smiles warmly up to me, eyes soft, her expression open. I'm not sure any man or woman has seen this side of her. Well, outside of Solana and Georgie at least.

"Hey," she says as I drape the towel over her shoulders. She sets her wet hands on my shoulders to balance on tiptoe and plants a kiss on my mouth.

That's another thing. I kissed her. And I find myself kissing her again now. I don't kiss women. Ever. I fuck them. We both get what we want out of it, and I leave. But Mercedes? Kissing is an intimacy I need like air when it comes to her. And if I'm not careful, she will destroy me.

Would it be some comfort to her to know this? I doubt it.

"Mercedes." I break our kiss.

She looks confused, a little hurt. But then she grins as her hand finds my erection, and with a groan, I drag her off.

"No."

"Really?" She raises her eyebrows.

I secure the towel around her and walk out of the bathroom to get her coffee and the small bag. She is wringing water from her long hair when I reenter.

"Coffee."

"That was thoughtful of you," she says, her eyes moving to the paper bag. Her hair tumbles down her back when she releases it to take the mug. "I'm thinking black tonight, by the way. What do you think?"

"Tonight?"

"Vivien's cocktail party." She rolls her eyes. "She's turning twenty-six."

"Oh. That's right. I'm sure you'll look lovely in anything you choose."

She gives me a look, then glances at the bag. "What's that?"

I take the pill out. There are more inside, but I set the bag on the counter as she looks at the plain packaging. Raul picked it up for me at a pharmacy out of town.

She raises her eyebrows, gaze wary now.

"Morning after pill. I wasn't careful with you."

It takes her a very long minute to drag her gaze to mine. Even then, she doesn't speak right away. She searches my eyes for something I can't give her.

"There are a few more in the bag. One should be enough, but to be safe…" I trail off.

"Oh. Okay, thanks, I guess." She takes the pill and sets it on the counter.

"Don't you want to take it?"

She forces a smile. "Are you going to watch me to be sure I do?"

"Mercedes, I came inside you. Multiple times."

"I know how it works, Judge. But I also know my cycle, and you don't have to worry." She shifts her gaze slightly as she says it, and suddenly, I am worried.

"Take the pill."

"You know I wouldn't trap you. That's not who I am," she says to her own reflection as she applies moisturizer to her face. I recognize Solana's label. I still have the bag she gave me on my bathroom counter.

I take her arm and turn her to me. "I won't let you ruin yourself."

She tugs out of my grasp with a snort. "Are you afraid Councilor Hildebrand will pin a scarlet A to my chest and make me stand on a scaffold in the courtyard? Shit, you know what? I wouldn't be surprised." She pops the pill out of its packaging and sets it on her tongue, then drinks a swallow of coffee. She opens her mouth to show me she swallowed it. "Satisfied?"

"This is for your own good, Mercedes."

"Because you'll never marry me."

"I'll never marry anyone."

"Can you go? I need some privacy."

I brush her cheek, but she pulls away from me. "I care about you. You know that, right?"

"I do, Judge." She turns to me. "You just don't care enough."

That cuts deep, but it's no less than I deserve. I open my mouth to speak, but the phone in my pocket dings with a message. I reach for it but catch myself because it's her phone. Mine is silenced. Mercedes rolls her eyes and turns away from me.

"You'd better get that. I'm sure it's important. Close the door on your way out."

"Mercedes—"

A second message makes it chime again. I walk out of her bedroom to dig the phone out and read the new texts.

Cunt, you see how easy it was to get close to you? That was a trial run. The big event will be much more... hands-on.

By the way, that girlfriend of yours is pretty smokin'. She should know better than to leave her windows unlocked. People are too trusting these days.

"Fuck!" I text Raul to bring the car around and dial Ezra as I climb in. "The apothecary," I tell Raul as Ezra answers.

"Judge? What is it?"

"Is security still in place for Solana and Georgie?"

"Yes, they've each got a man watching."

"And where are they? Where's Solana right now?"

"Just a minute," he says, and I hear him have another quick conversation before coming back on the line. "They're both at her shop." I'm guessing Solana and Georgie have figured out that I have soldiers watching them, but I'm not sure they realize why. As far as they know, what happened to Mercedes was an accident. I don't want to alarm anyone, but I'm also not taking any chances.

"You're sure?"

"I just confirmed. Why?"

"I want more men on them. And I need someone at Solana's house. I just received a text from our friend. He made a comment about her I don't like. We need to search the house. Make sure no one's been in there and make certain it's secure. We may need to change the locks."

"Have you discussed this with her?" Ezra asks cautiously.

"No, of course not."

"Do you think you should?"

I sigh. Christ. "Just get some men there and have a look around. I'll let her know about the locks."

"That's a good idea, Judge."

When we pull up to the apothecary, Georgie is just getting ready to leave. But when he sees me climbing out of the Rolls, he stops.

"What are you doing here?" he asks after peering into the car and seeing I'm alone.

Looking around, I note the man sitting in his sedan with its tinted windows across the street. When I turn back to Georgie, his eyebrows are raised.

"They're about as subtle as a UFO," he says.

After I glance up and down the street once more, I gesture to go in. "I need to talk to you two."

His expression grows serious, and we enter the shop where Solana is finishing up with a customer. She falters when she sees me, then smiles at the woman and locks the door behind her once she's gone.

"Is Mercedes okay?" she asks.

"Mercedes is fine." I see her as Douglas would for a moment. She's petite and would be easy to overpower. Georgie very clearly works out. And he has a toughness to him. He isn't a stranger to the streets. "Can we sit down?"

"Sure. Do you want coffee or something?"

I shake my head. "Mercedes doesn't know I'm here. I'd like to keep it that way." We sit at the same table as last time, and I remember that day. The terrible moments of powerlessness as her throat closed up.

"Judge? What the fuck is going on?" Georgie asks.

"The man who delivered those beignets, he thinks he knows Mercedes."

"What?" Solana asks.

"It was on purpose?" Georgie asks. "Someone hurt her on purpose?"

"You can't talk to her about this, do you understand? I don't want her scared."

"She has a right to know if she's in danger."

"She knows enough, and she's safe at the house. Outside of it, I won't let her out of my sight. But I'm here because of you." I look at Solana.

"Me?"

"In an effort to draw Mercedes out, I'm afraid this man may target you."

"Solana?" Georgie asks.

"I have men at your house now. We're taking a look around."

"What? He was at my house?"

"You're staying with me tonight and for the foreseeable future," Georgie says.

"I think that's a good idea," I tell Georgie.

"But—"

"I've increased security. I think it will be good for him to see the guards, so I'm sending more."

"More guards?" Solana says, and I have to remember she's not part of our world. She lives in a bubble of perceived safety.

Georgie, though, he just nods. He's not as carefree as he appears when the three of them are together.

"My house is alarmed," he says. "She'll be safe there."

"I'm not hiding away."

"You shouldn't. You should go on with your lives. It's Mercedes he wants. But I'd rather be on the safe side."

"Well, that's a first," Georgie says.

"What is?"

"I agree with you."

I smirk at him and turn to her. "Solana, if I can have a key to your house. I'll make sure the locks are good."

"What?"

"Here," Georgie takes a ring of keys out of his pocket. "This is Solana's. Her locks are shit. I've been telling her to change them for years."

I take the key.

"Who is he?" Solana asks.

"Just someone who thinks he can get something from her." They see the lie. But when Solana opens her mouth, Georgie puts an arm around her and tugs her close.

"He's been to my house?" she says again.

"Don't worry. Judge is right. Creeps like that guy are cowards. I'm sure he said it to get exactly this reaction," he says, but I know he is only doing it to reassure her, and I give him an infinitesimal nod.

I set two cards on the table. "This is my personal cell phone. You call if you see anything strange or need anything." I stand. "Not a word to Mercedes. Are we in agreement on that?"

They both nod.

"When can we see her?" Solana asks.

"We'll see." My phone rings. It's Ezra. "Call if you need anything. I will bring you the new keys myself later today."

"Thank you," Solana says. "I'm glad she has you to take care of her."

"I'm glad she has you for friends," I say before I can think about what I'm saying. They're as surprised as I am as I walk out the door and take Ezra's call.

14

JUDGE

When I get home that evening, Mercedes is dressed in a little black dress that she looks like she was poured into, along with five-inch heels. Her hair is twisted elegantly to one side and rests in thick waves over her shoulder.

For a moment, I'm confused about why she's dressed the way she is, but then I remember. The cocktail party. Vivien's birthday. I'd forgotten.

She turns to me. "You're late."

"I had some things I needed to take care of." We had to change the locks on both doors, repair two windows and update the locks on those too. There wasn't any evidence of a break-in, but it all took much longer than I expected.

"What things?"

"Business."

"What business?"

"Nothing. I'd better change."

"Nothing. Of course." She turns her back on me, her attention on the portrait of my grandparents and my father, and I wonder if she sees the similarities between my grandfather and me.

I leave the room, take a quick shower, and then get dressed. Black on black today. Mercedes is talking to Lois when I get downstairs. Lois greets me, then leaves us alone.

"What's going on, Judge?" she asks, taking the cuff link I can't seem to slip through the cuff and doing it for me. I watch her hands work with the dark red nails. The gloss of her hair on her bent head. A flash of memory steals my breath. Mercedes on her knees before me, naked, choking on my dick.

I close my eyes and think about something else. Anything else. But to have her this close, to smell the hint of perfume, feel her warmth, and have her do something so domestic as helping me with a cuff link, it's all a lot.

"Just work."

"Liar." She finishes with the link. "I don't want to stay long tonight. Maybe you can take me out to dinner after?"

"We'll see."

"I just have to show my face."

"I thought you liked these events. Everyone looking at you..."

She shrugs a shoulder, her mask of confidence faltering before she can turn away.

Stopping her, I tilt her chin up. "You don't have to go if you don't want to go."

"That's your world, Judge. Not mine."

"You just have to choose to make it yours. What do you care what they think of you anyway?"

"I don't. I just don't like people talking behind my back."

"I'll be there with you. I won't leave you alone."

She bites her lip. "Promise?"

"Promise."

I know all that's going on can't be easy and what she did still hangs over her head. No matter if we discuss it or not. I wonder what it will take to alleviate her guilt over the accidental murder. Because it was accidental, there's no doubt of that. And that woman was prepared to kill Santiago. Her death is no loss to the world. But she is dead. And Mercedes killed her.

Raul drives us while two more men follow in a second vehicle.

"How much longer with these guys?" she asks.

"Until Abel is caught." It's not a complete lie. I am worried about what Abel might do to Mercedes. He had no qualms about having Santiago dragged before The Tribunal and accused of the crimes Abel himself committed while his pregnant wife lay in a coma. I don't doubt he'd hurt Mercedes in any way he could. But Abel's been in Tribunal custody for about two months now. He can't get to her to hurt her physically. But she doesn't know that.

We arrive to a candlelit event at the IVI compound. The night is mild, so people are milling about outdoors as well as indoors, and as I guide Mercedes through the entrance, I feel the tightening of her muscles beneath my touch. She's steeling herself.

"I wasn't sure you were going to make it!" a woman's voice calls out as I hand Mercedes a flute of champagne. It's Vivien and beside her are her two friends, Giordana and Dulce. I don't remember any of their last names.

The three of them cross the courtyard drawing much attention as they sway their hips. They're dressed to kill with not much left to the imagination. They all glance at me, gazes skirting over me, devious smiles curling their pretty mouths. They're good looking, but this kind of woman has never attracted me.

"I wouldn't miss your birthday, Viv!" Mercedes says loudly as they air-kiss and lightly hug each other. "You are the pioneer, after all. Leading our little group into the next stage of life."

"I'd hardly call twenty-six the next stage. Besides, you're just a year behind me."'

"A year is a year. I'll take it. Oh! Before I forget." Mercedes reaches into her clutch and hands the woman a small Tiffany box. "Happy Birthday."

"Oh, you shouldn't have," Vivien says but greedily opens it to find a silver bracelet with baubles hanging from it. "It's gorgeous! Thank you." They air-kiss again, and I wonder how she stands it.

"You're welcome. They're from Judge and me." Mercedes tucks her arm into mine.

"Well, well," Dulce says. "So is it official?" She raises her eyebrows.

"Not yet. Not with all that's going on," Mercedes says, lowering her voice. I want to shake her. "My sister-in-law…"

"Oh, I know. We heard. How is dear Ivy?"

"The same."

"You haven't been to see her. Why not?" Giordana asks, and I wonder if Mercedes hears the note of cruelty in her voice. She's clearly too surprised by the question, though. I see that on her face. "My sister volunteers at the hospital. She knows all the comings and goings."

Fucking bitch.

"Well, I'm sure she missed Mercedes's visits then. You know how the De La Rosas keep odd hours," I say.

"Judge." I'm surprised to hear that voice. Although why am I surprised? "Excuse us," I tell the women and walk toward my mother, who smiles wide, and to anyone watching, I'm sure she looks thrilled to see us. "I didn't realize you'd be here."

"I'm escorting Mercedes, Mother. Nice to see you." I kiss her cheek as is customary. She'd pull away if we weren't at a Society event.

"I'd have offered Mercedes a ride if I'd known she was invited." She turns to Mercedes. "I know how much he hates these things. I'll take you home if he wants to leave early, dear."

"Thank you, Mrs. Montgomery. That's kind of you."

"Ah, just the man I wanted to see," Hildebrand says. He's clearly on his way out because he wouldn't be invited to this party.

"Councilor," I say.

"Ladies." He greets my mother and Mercedes both with a kiss on the hand. "Might I borrow Judge Montgomery for a moment? I promise not to keep him long."

I don't want to go, but I know I can't refuse. My mother takes Mercedes's arm. "Let's go mingle, shall we?"

"Let's." Mercedes meets my eyes only briefly before slipping into the crowd, and I turn to Hildebrand.

Hildebrand's expression darkens as the women leave. "I'm sorry to interrupt your evening, but I was on my way to your house, so this saves me a trip."

"My house? Why? Not that you're not welcome, of course."

We walk toward The Tribunal building, ascending the curving stairs toward his office. From the window, I see the scaffold outside. It's unlit but no less eerie. This courtyard is only visible from The Tribunal building. Even the sounds of the party just on the other side of the walls don't penetrate here.

"Scotch?" Hildebrand asks when we enter his office.

"Sure." He pours for both of us, then takes his seat behind the desk. I sit across from him and hold his gaze as he watches me. Hildebrand studied law, like me. He was a judge in the outside world, like I am. I know he sees me following in his footsteps and becoming a councilor of The Tribunal at some point.

"Abel Moreno has made some accusations against Ms. De La Rosa to The Tribunal privately."

"Oh? What accusations?"

"That she was involved with his plan to use the courtesan to poison her brother."

"Did he say that?"

Hildebrand nods.

"Well, I can tell you without a doubt that Mercedes would never hurt her brother. She loves him dearly. He's the only family she has left. And you and I are both aware that Abel accused Santiago of all the crimes he himself is guilty for. Not to mention others."

"True. What is another lie to a liar?" He pauses. I keep my gaze level. "You know, the courtesan seems to have disappeared."

"Has she?"

"Her apartment has been cleared out meticulously."

"Oh?"

"Yes, too meticulous, if you ask me."

"I didn't realize."

He takes a drink, letting the silence hang. "I hear Ms. De La Rosa hasn't been to see her sister-in-law in the hospital. Why is that?" No segue into this change of topic then.

"I haven't allowed it. I feel it would be too upsetting for all of them."

"Because the relationship within the family is strained. Hence The Rite."

"With all due respect, what are you getting at, Councilor?"

Silence again. I won't crack, and he knows it. But it doesn't stop him in his little power play. After an eternity, he smiles and shakes his head. "I'm sure it's nothing. That young woman surely isn't capable of doing anything that may cause harm to others."

"Surely not."

"Well, anyway, I was going to ask you where your brother is. Your mother told me you knew, but she couldn't say."

Goddamn bitch.

"Why are you looking for Theron?"

"I've had a call from a family in our Washington faction. Seems there may be a match for him."

"Is that so?"

"Unless, of course, Ms. De La Rosa and he—"

"Ms. De La Rosa and he are not an item."

He smiles and nods. "And your intentions with the young lady?"

"Excuse me?"

"You should know there are rumors. I know your reputation, Judge. You are above reproach. Just take care. You know how cruel some can be."

"I do." Hildebrand included.

"Good. Now since I have you, if you don't mind, talk through a case with me, will you? I could use some sage advice."

"Of course," I say, although all I want to do is get back to the party, where I promised I wouldn't leave Mercedes on her own, and whisk her away before those vultures can do any more damage. Because they have been talking, stirring up things they have no business in. But more than an hour passes before I return to the courtyard. Guests have grown louder as they drink, and more of them have gathered in the courtyard, but Mercedes isn't among them.

That's when I see my mother. Well, I hear her first. Her laugh is too shrill. I walk to where she's speaking with a group of mostly middle-aged men, and I wonder if she is looking for a new match. It would make sense. When she sees me, she misses a beat but is quick to cover it up with a smile toward me.

"Mother."

"Judge. Don't tell me Councilor Hildebrand kept you this long. How gauche!"

"Have you seen Mercedes?"

"She was dancing a little while ago." I stiffen, and she smiles wide. "Inside."

"Thank you," I say tightly and walk toward the French doors that lead inside. Classical music pours from the Baroque room where an orchestra plays. People stop me as I weave through the crowd. I am polite but brief, and I hear her before I spot her, and I swear every fucking muscle in my body tenses.

Someone says something to me, but I barely hear him before pushing past and stalking onto the dance floor where Mercedes is in the arms of a young man, a Sovereign Son no less. She stumbles, and they both laugh, and for a moment, I wonder if she's drunk. If they're both fucking drunk. But whatever he's saying must be the funniest thing she's ever heard because she throws her head back and laughs. That man—that fucking man—has the gall to brush his lips over her throat, and I think I'm going to kill him. Right here, in the middle of this room with all these witnesses, I'm going to fucking kill him.

Mercedes sees me just as I get to them. Her eyes flicker in panic momentarily, then something else. Something stubborn and arrogant, and I remember her face when I gave her the pill this morning. I remember the hurt I saw there, followed by the shutting of the door.

And I know what this is. She's teaching me a lesson.

I also know I have no right to do what I'm about to do. But I close my hand over the man's shoulder and squeeze. "Excuse me," I say, eyes locked on her.

"What the—?"

The look on my face must say it all because as soon as I glance his way, he releases her, raising both arms into the air in surrender. I set my hand on Mercedes's lower back and tug her to me.

"What the fuck do you think you're doing?"

"What the fuck do you think you're doing?" she

asks. I take in the flush of her cheeks and the loudness of her laughter moments ago.

"Are you drunk?"

"Where were you? Cat House? Is it open for business tonight?"

I tighten my grip on her. "Are you fucking drunk?"

She grins. "I'm not, actually. It would take more than a sip of champagne to get drunk. I'm just enjoying myself, Judge. And what do you care? You don't want me. You've made that abundantly clear. You just want to be sure I take that little pill to erase your mistake."

I glance around to see eyes on us. "It wasn't a mistake," I tell her quietly. "We're leaving."

"I don't want to leave. You go. Your mom said she'd take me home."

I lean in close to her. "Oh, little monster, that wasn't a request. And you just wait until I get you home."

15

MERCEDES

Judge's mood is a dark, palpable thing for the entirety of the ride home. More than once, I feel his gaze on the side of my face as I stare out the window. I don't give him the satisfaction of a response, even when his palm settles on my thigh, sliding up just beneath the hem of my dress. The warmth of his touch brands his possession into my skin, and if I wasn't so raw from his earlier rejection, I might find it amusing.

We pull into the drive, and he helps me from the car with all the practiced elegance of a refined, well-bred man. This is how the world sees Lawson Montgomery, but beneath it all, I can't help thinking what a hypocrite he is. He wears his finery to cover up his depravity, the same as me. Beneath those suits is a man who takes pleasure in ruining me, all while his lips spew lies about giving me away to someone else. Lurking under that veneer he presents to the world is a beast. A beast whose eyes I've stared into while he's threatened to harm me, all while the echo of his promise to protect me fades away.

I wonder if he ever tires of it, these dueling personalities. I know how exhausting it is to live this way, and I'm only twenty-five. He's been doing this for thirty-one years, and he still hasn't chosen a side.

"Thank you for tonight." I pull my hand from his the moment I step out. "It's always such a pleasure to see you in your natural habitat."

"Mercedes." He calls after me with a growl as I walk into the house, my heels echoing off the floor.

I ignore him, but I can feel his presence behind me. His eyes burn into my back as I traverse the stairs and enter the corridor leading to his bedroom. Deftly, I reach behind me and unzip my dress before I even reach his door, clutching the fabric to my naked breasts. As soon as I step inside, I let it fall from my body, kicking it off before I bend over and strip my thong off too.

Judge's polished shoes come to a dead halt as he enters behind me, taking in the scene. I glance over my shoulder and offer him another fake smile. The same one I reserve for everyone else. Today, when Judge made his position clear, I decided it's time to let go of my ridiculous notions.

This game between us has very real stakes, and it's been easy to forget in the thick of it. But the battle lines have been drawn, and in the end, I'm the one who will have to face the consequences.

When I leave this house and his care, Judge will go back to the life he knows. He will spend his days at work, serving his purpose for The Society, and his nights will be spent in the comfort of a warm body that isn't mine.

In my time here, I've grasped at every justification for my jealousy and the unwarranted possession I feel toward him. He was my first, but I'm not his, and I certainly won't be his last. He wants a life free from complications, and I can't forget that, even in the face of his temporary control. This flame of passing desire will inevitably burn out for him, and we will part ways.

I know there's no guarantee I'll go unscathed. Truthfully, I know I won't. I've already given him more of me than I've ever given anyone else. I've made the mistake of letting him in and letting my guard down. But if I'm to survive this, I have to separate the two. I have to learn how to give him my body without giving him my heart.

"We need to talk about your little performance at the party," he says.

I toss my thong to the floor and leave my heels on, turning to face him. His eyes burn a slow path down my naked body, the vein in his neck pulsing with the betrayal of his need. I move toward him slowly, and he eyes me with suspicion as I unbutton his suit jacket and slide my palms inside over his chest.

"Haven't you heard?" I tip my chin up to peer into his eyes. "I'm in want of a husband."

He stiffens, but I don't acknowledge it as I push his coat back over his broad shoulders and divest him of it entirely.

"I figure there really shouldn't be any wasted opportunities," I add, my fingers moving over the buttons of his vest, slipping them through the holes. "I'm not getting any younger, and the longer this ruse goes on, the more people will start to question it."

"You mean the way they question it when you willingly tell them it's official." He arches a dark brow at me.

"That was just to goad Vivien." I shrug. "She can't stand the idea of it."

"Yes, and she likes to gossip." He studies me sharply as I help him from his vest and move onto his button-down shirt.

"Don't worry." I stare straight at his chest, proud of how empty my voice is as I give him my assurances. "It's always the woman's reputation that falls into question. Yours will go unscathed, as a Sovereign Son."

"Mercedes." His voice is quieted as he tries to

still my hand, but I shove his away and keep working to undress him.

"In all honesty, though, I really don't think it will matter too much. As you saw tonight, Clifton Phillips had no issue with my reputation as he took me for a spin around the dance floor. I think he could be husband material. He's a little arrogant, but I suppose everyone has their faults."

"Are we back to this again?" Judge sighs, but it quickly turns to frustration when I look up at him deadpan.

"I'm not joking," I tell him. "I know the whole purpose of me coming here to stay with you was to reform me, but let's not kid ourselves. I am who I am. They may have broken the mold with me when it came to creating a perfect Society wife, but it doesn't negate the fact I still need to wed. I have a legacy to carry on. A duty to the De La Rosa name."

Irritation pinches his features, and I almost wish I could believe it means something. But I'm not falling into that honey pot again.

"Let's not make this complicated." I toss his shirt aside and reach for the zipper of his trousers. "It's time for me to grow the fuck up, right? And don't get me wrong, I enjoy this. I really, really enjoy this. But at some point, preferably soon, I'll find someone else to take over the responsibility of my care and free you from the burden you've shouldered for far too long already."

He reaches for my wrist, squeezing it in his palm before I can yank down his briefs. "What the hell is wrong with you?"

"What do you mean?" I stare at him, blank.

"This." He gestures back at me. "It's like you've been reprogrammed. You're acting as dead inside as your friends tonight."

"It's the bane of being a Society princess." I lift my shoulder daintily, but he doesn't seem amused.

We stare at each other in tense silence, unspoken truths blooming in the space between us. I could pretend to guess what his might be, but I won't. If he wanted to say them, he would.

"I don't like you like this," he says finally, his tone too acidic to be mistaken for anything else.

"I'm sorry. Was that too much honesty for you?"

When he doesn't reply, I slide my free hand down between my thighs, toying with myself while he watches.

"I didn't intend for this to turn into a therapy session. In fact, that's the last thing I want. So are you going to participate, or are you going to watch? Either way, I'm getting off tonight."

He releases my hand and grabs me by the face, his thumb dragging over my lips. His eyes are half reverence, half regret. But we aren't going back to that place. I prove it when I stop playing with myself and thread my fingers through the belt loops of his trousers, tugging him forward.

He doesn't fight me as I pull him to the chair and shove him down into it roughly, only to climb atop him and straddle him. His eyes are liquid fire when I reach between us, and this time, there are no protests from his lips when I drag his cock free from his trousers.

My stomach clenches as I stroke him in my palm, our eyes locked, our breaths mingling. I want to know what he's thinking, but I don't dare ask. Instead, I lean my body into his, capturing his lips with mine as I feed his cock into me slowly. So slowly, it's impossible to miss the catch in his breath when I drag my fingers through his hair and tilt his head back, biting my way down his jaw and neck.

Judge groans, and I do it again because I want to play that sound on repeat. His palms come to rest on my ass, squeezing me as I start to rock against him. When I leave a bite mark on his neck, branding him in the only way I can, he snaps his gaze back to mine. His nostrils flare, and he yanks me down against him hard, forcing me to bear the full brutality of his cock. And I know he's let me have my fun when his palm slaps my ass, reverberating with a sharp crack.

"This isn't a game, little monster." He wraps a

handful of hair into his fist, keeping my gaze pinned to his as he fucks me from below.

"No?" I whisper. "Then what is it?"

In answer, he fucks me harder. Faster. Smacking my ass and grunting out the frustrations he refuses to give voice to. He has no fucking reason to be pissed off, yet that's exactly what he is.

"If this is what you call punishment, maybe I should misbehave more often," I muse.

"Punishment?" he growls. "How's this for punishment?"

He stands up and unceremoniously dumps me onto the floor, fisting his cock inches from my face as he glares down at me. What he's doing would be hot in any other circumstance, but there's no pleasure in it. He's choking the life out of his cock, his anger driving home his point that he will deny me what I want. I know it when he grabs me by the hair and holds me there, forcing an orgasm as his come spurts over my breasts before dripping down onto my thighs.

He releases me with a ragged breath and glares down at me. "Little brats don't get to come."

"Little brats make themselves come." I thrust my fingers between my thighs resentfully, and he turns away, stalking toward the door.

There's no pleasure in my actions, not with his abrupt dismissal, and I refuse to let him walk away from this so easily.

"So how does this work exactly?" I call after him. "How much was my time worth to you just now? Will you leave some cash on the floor beside me before you go?"

He freezes, his back going rigid, but he doesn't turn around. He doesn't say a goddamned word.

"Or do you consider this a bonus?" I ask. "On top of what Santiago's already paying you."

His head dips, the only sign he even heard me, but again, I get no response. The silence goes on too long. It's too painful. And despite my best efforts to restore myself to factory defaults, wipe away all my emotions, I revert to the mess he's made of me.

"Clifton asked me out on a date, and I want to go. Next week."

"No." The word squeezes through what I don't doubt are clenched teeth.

"It's not up to you." I force myself to remain calm. "I need to find a husband, and I'm tired of waiting. There's nothing to be accomplished by you keeping me locked up here—"

"I said no!" he roars.

The thunder in his voice silences me, but if that wasn't effective enough, he takes it a step further, snatching a decorative vase from the nearest table. When he hurls it at the wall, shattering it with a deafening blow, I can't help but flinch.

Slowly, he turns his sharp gaze to me, and at that moment, I hardly recognize the man I know burning beneath the hatred in his eyes. But for a moment, only a fleeting moment, I see something else there too. Something that looks like the same agony I feel splitting my ribs apart.

"Over my dead body," he grits out. "Will you ever go out with him."

With that final blow, he prowls from the room entirely, slamming the door behind him.

I SMEAR my fingers through the come on my chest while my empty reflection stares back at me from the mirror. For three minutes, my thoughts have swung wildly on a pendulum, trying to decide if this is the evidence of his hatred or his possession. But in the end, it doesn't matter. One is the short road to heartbreak, and the other is the long. The result, inevitably, will always be the same.

I wash him off me, tears stinging my eyes as I reach for my makeup bag and dig through it with trembling fingers. When I pinch the pill between my fingers, examining the only evidence I need to understand, something inside me breaks all over again.

I had given myself a long list of reasons I couldn't really swallow it this morning. At first, I had even managed to convince myself it was the Catholic in me that led me to employ the sleight of hand Judge never saw coming. It was something I practiced many times over the years with Antonia when she'd force us to take the pain pills after our father's beatings. Back then, I didn't think I deserved anything to dull the pain if I had earned it in the first place. It was the stubborn De La Rosa in me, and in my own way, I thought I'd be more righteous for refusing any comfort. But this pill wasn't designed for comfort. I knew it the moment Judge pulled it from the packaging. I felt shameful, like something wrong he needed to blot from his memory. But when I settled my palm over my belly after he left the room, I knew I couldn't erase it. The thought was unbearable to me, and I couldn't bring myself to admit that in front of him.

I'd made a decision, standing in the bathroom alone this morning. It was a decision that might alter my life irrevocably. And I didn't know how I felt so certain of it already, but I did. There weren't many things I'd ever been sure of in my life. But I knew when I pressed my hand to flesh, there was something inside me I couldn't regret.

As I stand here now, even with tears burning my eyes, my feelings haven't changed. I never wanted to be someone's throwaway. I'm not even convinced that I'd ever really wanted to be a wife before I could imagine a husband worthy of my love. But there is one thing I have always ached for. One desire I knew I'd never be able to give up. That was a child. A family of my own. Even if that family only consists of me and my son or daughter.

My resolve is unwavering when I force my gaze back to the mirror. I know what it might cost me. I'm aware my reputation will be ruined, and my brother will probably disown me. And Judge... well, Judge will hate me until the day I die. But this is my cross to bear, and I will do it on my own. I will do it without shame or regret, and I will do it with enough love in my heart to eclipse the absence of anyone else by my side.

"That is my promise." I close my eyes on a whisper, letting a solitary tear fall before I walk to the toilet, dump the pill into the bowl, and flush it away.

It's a promise I refuse to break.

16

MERCEDES

In the aftermath of our fight, days pass, eventually turning into weeks. During that time, Judge and I revert to what we know best. He loses himself in his work and whatever else he's been hiding from me. At night, he sneaks into the bedroom once he thinks I'm asleep to lay on his side and leave before I wake. There have been several times when I felt him turn toward me, his hand hovering just above my arm or hip. Once, he even brushed the hair back from my face. But he hasn't taken it further, and I suspect he may actually hold himself to it this time. It's a gut-wrenching realization, but at the same time, I know we're both too stubborn to give in.

He hasn't outright told me what the rules are or why guards are hovering about the property outside, but instead uses them as his carrier pigeons, delivering grunted messages that I'm not allowed out. I'm imprisoned again for reasons he doesn't think I need to know, and my only contact with the outside world is the phone he gave me, which I'm fairly certain is linked to his. I don't doubt he can see everything on it, so I have to be careful what I say or do, but I know with every passing day, it's time to seriously consider my options.

The first and most viable option is to approach my brother, but right now that's not even possible with the current circumstances. I've been texting him occasionally for reports on Ivy and the baby, and he's given me terse replies. At least, that was until last week, when he sent me a message to inform me the baby had been born healthy, and she was being well cared for. It was a happy and sad moment as I stared at the first photo of my niece from a screen. But the news wasn't all good because when I asked, there was still no improvement with Ivy. I didn't have to hear Santiago's voice to feel his heartbreak. What started as a war had evolved to something else, and in my present circumstances, I can finally understand that.

I feel remorse for the way I've treated Ivy. I feel partially responsible for what happened to her too. And I wish more than anything I hadn't held on to my anger for so long. Being where I am now, I can see things through a different lens. I can see her humanity, her fragility, and the simple truth is that she and I aren't all that different. We are both trapped in a world we've been trying to navigate the only way we know how. Her captor was my brother, and mine is Judge. And despite all odds, Santi has developed feelings for her. Feelings I have no doubt are love. I feel it's only fair that one of us gets their happy ending, and I find myself praying every day for her recovery so that it can be her.

Meanwhile, I'm still trying to figure out what the hell I'm going to do. I've considered contacting Clifton. When I told Judge I needed to find a husband, I wasn't just goading him. The thought entered my mind more than a few times already that I can only make the best of the situation I'm in. I'm a hostage to The Society until I can either convince Santi to give me my portion of the inheritance I'm owed or find someone to marry me. Judge has made it clear it won't be him, and if I truly intend to protect myself, I can't allow him to find out what I've done.

Like in any other hostage situation, the only way out is through negotiation. Clifton is a Sovereign Son, but he's unwed because he's looking for an affluent wife to pad his bank account. The Phillips line isn't nearly as wealthy as the De La Rosas, and my dowry is undoubtedly a shiny, bright beacon to him. He isn't at all romantic, and I realize now that I shouldn't be either. We can make a business deal. I could tell him the truth about my situation, and he would agree to it because the benefit to him outweighs any feelings he might have about my circumstances. We could have a shotgun wedding, sign the contract, and live in harmony as roommates who are free to do as they please with nobody being any wiser.

It all sounds good in theory, but as I type out a draft message to the phone number I'd hidden in my clutch, I'm still not convinced I can bring myself to do it. A wave of nausea rolls over me at the prospect of bearing his family crest on my neck. It feels like a betrayal, a hot knife to the heart. But what choice do I have?

I write the text over and over again, rewording it, trying to remain vague but interested as I propose we have a conversation at the next Society event two weeks from now. There's no guarantee I'll actually be able to sneak off to do that, but I'll have to try if I really plan to follow through with this. The alternative is being locked up like a prisoner with a man who runs so hot and cold that he'll never agree to my release or my capture.

"Fucking hell." I toss the phone aside with a sigh and collapse onto the bed. "It shouldn't be this hard."

"Everything okay, dear?" Lois pops her head

through the doorway, and I glance up at her with a smile.

"Yes, of course. I'm just... having a moment."

"We all do." Her eyes crinkle with amusement. "Your friends are here for afternoon tea."

"Oh." I spring up eagerly. "Thank you so much."

She beams at my eagerness, the first she's seen in days. I've been sleeping far too much and have been less than excited about all the delicious food she prepares, which I feel guilty about. But I just haven't felt like myself.

Getting up, I follow Lois out the doorway and down to the sitting room, where Solana and Georgie are waiting for me. They're studying the cute little towers of pastries and finger sandwiches Lois has prepared for today, quietly bickering about who gets what.

"There are plenty more in the kitchen," Lois assures them with a laugh before she takes her leave. "I always make way too much."

They thank her, and their gazes snap to me as I join them.

"Hey." Solana pulls me in for a hug first, followed by Georgie, who then holds me at arm's length.

"Are you okay?"

"Of course." I force a smile. "Why wouldn't I be?"

He bites his lip in that way he does when he's concerned. "You just... look a little pale."

"It's nothing." I wave it off. "I've just been feeling bleh this week."

"Well, you're going to love this creepy-ass gift from Madame Dubois then." Solana chuckles as she hands me a brown paper bag. "She insisted I must bring this to you."

"Oh, God, what is it?" I peek inside and take a sniff.

"Ginger tea," Solana informs me. "She said she had a feeling you'd need it."

"Huh?" I murmur, my brow furrowing.

"I'm telling you, that woman scares the bejeezus out of me." Georgie shudders. "I kid you not, last week she brought me a box of Band-Aids. Two hours later, I sliced my thumb clean open with a pair of shears."

"Told you she was the real deal." Solana snorts. "And here everyone thought I was crazy for bringing her into the shop."

"Well, please thank her for me." I set the tea aside absently.

"Okay, can we dig in?" Georgie's eyes drift back to the food. "I'm starving."

Solana and I laugh in acknowledgment, and we all fill our plates with entirely too much. I'm not even that hungry, but it all looks amazing, and I don't want to hurt Lois's feelings when she went to the trouble of doing this. Regardless, I'm fairly certain Georgie will eat the whole damned display himself if we let him.

We sit down and start to chatter between bites when a big glob of mayonnaise from one of the sandwiches squishes from the bread into my mouth and makes my stomach roil. Solana pauses, her macaron halfway to her lips.

"Are you okay?"

I nod, but another wave of nausea rolls over me, and I know I'm definitely not. I barely have the grace to set the plate aside without spilling the contents before I'm up on my feet and running to the nearest bathroom, where I proceed to puke my guts out.

I'm clinging to the toilet seat, my head a sweaty mess when I hear Solana's voice behind me.

"Oh, God," she chokes out. "The ginger tea..."

I blink up at her, too weak to deny my current reality.

"You have to swear you won't tell anyone," I beg. "Not even Georgie. Not yet, okay?"

Her eyes go wide, and she looks like she might be sick too. "Does Judge... I mean... are you sure?"

"Pretty sure." I whimper as another wave of nausea steals my breath. "But I'll need you to bring me a test this week and then take it away when you leave again."

She looks at me uncertainly. "Shouldn't you see a doctor?"

"I can't." I shake my head. "I just need some time."

"Okay," she whispers. "I'll do it. I'll figure something out."

"Thank you." I squeeze my eyes shut and focus on breathing. "It turns out I might need that tea after all."

17

JUDGE

I am divided.

Ever since Vivien's party and our fight, I've spent my days at the office only coming home to sleep and often not even that. The couch in my office is doubling as a makeshift bed.

It feels as though Mercedes and I are on repeat. Reliving the same hell over and over again. Sexually, I've never been as attracted to a woman as I am her. And attraction doesn't begin to cover it. She has this strange power over me. Something I can't seem to resist. And the things I do when I'm with her or near her—it's like all these years I've worked so hard to maintain control, to be the man everyone knows, they just go out the window.

I care about her, but it's not that simple. Nothing is with her. My feelings for her run deeper than simply caring for the sister of my best friend.

These are feelings I should not have. I want her in ways I cannot want her.

Because every time I touch her, I lose a little more of myself to the darkness inside me. I should give her up, but I can't. The thought of another man touching her, having her, brings about a violence inside me that burns so fucking hot its ferociousness scares even me.

We are what we are, all of us. No matter how we try to hide beneath what we show the world. And maybe it's just a matter of time until we give in to the depravity of our true selves.

I arrive home in the afternoon on the day Mercedes is having her friends over for high tea. I wasn't planning to return to the house, but Ezra called and insisted it was time to visit with my brother, and I decided perhaps I should go. I will need to deal with him at some point, and now is as good a time as any. So I've come to pack. At least I can use the excuse that she'll be busy with her friends to not see her. It's cowardice, I know, but I can't trust myself around her.

I enter through the back door, greet Lois briefly in the kitchen, and let her know I'll be out of town for the next two nights.

"You should say hello to Mercedes and her friends. They're having tea. That way, you can let her know so she's not disappointed."

I make a point of checking the time. "I'll miss my flight."

"Judge—"

"She won't be disappointed, Lois. She'll be happy."

"If you say so, Judge." She returns to the work of preparing finger sandwiches.

I don't overthink it. Instead, I walk quickly past the room they're in, ignoring their laughter, and head upstairs to my bedroom, where I take a small bag out of my closet and set it on the bed, which hasn't yet been made since Mercedes is sleeping in longer these days. I begin the task of packing the things I need. I'm just zipping the duffel when I see Mercedes's phone tossed on the bed.

I have her phone linked to mine so I can see all the text messages she sends as well as know the numbers she dials. So far, it's only been Georgie, Solana, and Santiago, and there's nothing out of the ordinary. I'm about to set the phone on top of the nightstand so it doesn't get lost in the mess of blankets when my thumb brushes the screen. There is no password. That was a requirement when I gave her this. And when I touch it, it lights up, and I see a message she is in the process of writing.

I really had a lovely time dancing with you at Vivien's party. I'd love to see you again at the next dinner. Perhaps we can talk without interruption then. There is something I'd like to discuss but

That's where it ends. Like she was interrupted.

My blood goes cold as I re-read the message. I check the phone number. It's saved under C. I almost roll my eyes as I compare the number to the one I have for Clifton Phillips in my own contact list.

Did she think she'd do this behind my back? Arrange some meeting? There is a dinner in two weeks at the compound that she and I will both need to attend. What the hell does she think she's going to discuss? Their date? I know he'd asked her out, but I thought I made it perfectly clear she'd go on a date with him over my dead body.

And Clifton Phillips. Like he's man enough to handle her.

I force a deep breath in as my own phone dings with a message from Ezra telling me the private plane will be ready to take off in one hour. I type out a response that I need to delay by a few days.

The three dots start bouncing as Ezra types out his response, telling me I shouldn't put it off much longer, that a brother is a brother, and that Theron is sorry, but that he'll stand by for word from me to rebook the flight. I wonder if he's so concerned about my relationship with Theron because he is estranged from his.

I ask about the thugs and the men they lead back to in Italy, and he tells me he's working on an agreement with them. Money talks. Always.

I thank him, then scroll to Clifton Phillips and hit the call button to invite him for dinner that same night. It takes all I have to do it. To swallow down my own resistance. And I'm not even sure why I'm doing it.

No, that's not true. It's to show her how poor a match he'd make.

If only my intentions were good, though. If only it was for her sake and not my own need to possess her, knowing all along I can never truly have her.

Setting my duffel back in the closet, I go downstairs, still avoiding Mercedes and her friends, and inform Lois that I will be home for dinner after all and that we will have a guest. I also ask her to instruct Mercedes to wear the dress I left out for her.

Later that evening, when I enter my bedroom, I find Mercedes trying to clasp the diamond necklace I sent over into place. I'm not sure why I bought it for her. She pauses when she sees me, her eyes meeting mine in the mirror over my dresser. The sight is so domestic. We're sharing a bedroom. She's in the middle of getting dressed. To anyone who doesn't know our situation, we could be husband and wife.

She blinks away first and curses when the necklace slips through her fingers and drops to the floor. It falls beside her sandals. They match the white gold dress with its spaghetti straps and a plunging neckline that dips to the waist giving one a glimpse of the roundness of her breasts. From the fitted waist, the soft fabric of the skirt drapes past her knees but has a long slit along the front of one thigh. I'm sure Clifton Phillips will start drooling the moment he sees her.

"I don't know what the hell you think you're doing," she says as we both bend to pick up the necklace. I get to it first. We straighten, and I'm standing too close. But I don't move.

"You seemed to enjoy Clifton's company at Vivien's birthday party, and I've considered what you said. And you're right. You are in need of a husband."

Her eyes are cold. Better than flat, like a Stepford wife. "I believe the exact words you used were over my dead body will you ever go out with him."

"Hmm." I look at the diamond necklace that cost a small fortune. I thought of her the instant I saw the woman setting it in the window of the exclusive jeweler I pass on my way to the courthouse. A delicate pavé-set diamond choker suspending a line of ten round diamonds. It's one of a kind. Like her. I brush her hair over her shoulder, the heat of her skin sending an electric jolt through me.

"I can do it myself." She tries to snatch the necklace.

"Be still." I brush my thumb over the IVI tattoo on the back of her neck and feel the empty space above it. Would I ever really allow Phillips to put his mark on here? The thought makes bile rise in my throat as I place the choker around her neck.

"Can you make up your mind what you want at least?" she asks.

Once I secure the necklace, I lift her hair and set it down her back, inhaling the clean scent of her shampoo, the hint of her signature perfume beneath it.

"You look beautiful."

She turns to face me. I still don't move, and she has to tilt her head way back, so she sets one hand against the dresser at her back to slip on her sandals, then look up at me. They add five inches, but she still has to crane her neck.

"I hope Clifton likes the dress. I'll make sure he knows you chose it for him," she taunts, and I don't have to shift my gaze from hers to see how her fingers play over the exposed skin of her thigh.

I grit my teeth and force a smile.

She steps around me. "I'm keeping the necklace, by the way."

"It's a gift. Of course, you are. And thank you is appropriate."

"Oh, I'm not sure I'd classify it as a gift. I think I more than earned it, don't you?"

I close the space between us, twirl a lock of thick, soft hair around my finger, then tilt her chin up. "Thank me."

She licks her lips and searches my face. "How would you like me to thank you, your honor? On my knees?" She reaches a hand to cup the crotch of my pants, and I grab her wrist, my breath hissing. "You'll ruin my makeup."

"You really think a man like Clifton Phillips can handle you? You'd eat him alive."

She grins, pleased. "Better that than him eating me, don't you think? Although…" I feel myself tense. Feel the heat of possessive jealousy begin to burn inside me. I squeeze her wrist.

"Relax, Judge." She giggles. "No one's eating anyone tonight." Pulling free, she turns and walks out of the bedroom, not bothering to close the door. I listen to her heels click as she steps down the stairs.

Clifton Philips arrives right on time, and Lois shows him into the living room, where I watch from my place by the fireplace, my arm resting against the stone mantel. Mercedes smiles her

Society smile. That's what I'm calling it from now on. It's one she gives all of them. Not me, though. This one she doesn't insult me with. And as Clifton shines in her light, I hold that thought.

This is for show. I get the real Mercedes.

But I find it hard nonetheless to greet him as he comes to shake my hand and thank me for the invitation.

Clifton Phillips is twenty-four years old. Younger than Mercedes. He's the firstborn of three Phillips sons. He comes from a Founding Family, although their fortunes have declined over the last decade or so. They still have money, but it's nothing to the De La Rosa or Montgomery fortunes. I wonder how much that has to do with the attention and compliments he pours over Mercedes. Her inheritance would bolster the Phillips's. Give him a nice cushion.

I put that thought aside. Mercedes is smart. She has her own agenda with Clifton, and of the two of them, I know he's the one I should worry about. As I sip my scotch, I consider how good my invitation to Clifton will look. As Mercedes's guardian, I have invited this man into my home to court her. I already mentioned it to my mother so I can be sure news will travel to Hildebrand and throughout The Society. It should at least dispel some of the rumors circulating about us.

The two of them share a private joke, and I

catch the seductive way Mercedes has of looking at men. She casts that thick-lashed glance at me while setting her hand on Clifton's knee. I know I am her target. I swallow a little more scotch, my hand a jealous fist around the crystal. "I believe dinner is ready," I say, gesturing to the dining room.

"Your home is beautiful, Judge," Clifton says as Mercedes shimmies her sweet round ass ahead of us. I catch Clifton's too eager gaze on it even as he speaks to me.

I wait to respond, and when he realizes I've caught him, he clears his throat, face flushing with embarrassment. "Thank you, Clifton." I set my hand on his shoulder a little too heavily. "She is lovely, isn't she? Hard not to look. But she is a Society daughter. And I don't want to see your eyes on her ass again, am I clear?"

"Yes, sir."

Sir. Christ. What a fucking pussy.

"Coming?" Mercedes asks from the entrance to the dining room.

I pat Clifton's back hard enough that he jerks forward.

Mercedes gives me a look as he passes her into the dining room.

I shrug a shoulder and take my place at the head of the table. I've set Mercedes to my right. Clifton is at the foot.

"You know what? I'll move down here with you," Mercedes tells Clifton, asking Lois to reset her place beside Clifton's. Lois looks at me, and I reluctantly nod. Although I admit it was childish to set him there. Like putting him at the kid's table.

The table seats a dozen, and I watch the two of them talk at the far end, only including me in bits and pieces of conversation. Clifton is clearly uncomfortable with the attention Mercedes is bestowing upon him. Between leaning her breasts to practically rest on the table and her hand disappearing beneath it to, I'm sure, his knee and it had better only be his fucking knee, he keeps glancing my way, face flushing with a combination of too much wine and a healthy fear of me.

"So Clifton," I say, putting my knife and fork down once I'm finished with the main course. I notice Mercedes hasn't eaten much. Is she trying to impress him? Or did I misread her, and she's fucking nervous around this idiot? She also hasn't touched her wine.

"Yes, sir," Clifton says.

"How is school going? You're still on track to graduate this year?" Clifton is studying law, and from what I've learned, he's nowhere near the top of his class, but he is very popular socially. I get it. He's good looking. And likes to party. I wonder if Mercedes is aware of how much.

"Yes, Judge. I'll be joining the family firm upon

graduation. Perhaps you'll see me in your courtroom someday soon."

Oh, joy. "Well, I'm sure your father is very proud of you."

"He is. And now that I'm readying to enter the next phase of life." He turns to Mercedes, and when his hand disappears beneath the table, it makes my own clench. "Well, let's just say I'm very glad to have run into Mercedes at the party."

"You know, Judge, Clifton and I were at a joint summer camp back when we were kids," Mercedes says. "Remember that?" she asks Clifton, setting her elbow on the table and turning her head so her hair forms a curtain between us. It's done to exclude me. I will remember it once he leaves.

He points at her, mouth going from an O to a wide grin as he remembers. "The canoe incident. That was you, wasn't it? We all suspected."

Mercedes sits back in her chair, opens her arms wide, and takes a small bow with a tilt of her head.

"That Mrs. Crotch deserved a good dunk."

"Mrs. Crotch. I can't even remember her real name. Can you?"

They both laugh at the memory.

"Now the skinny-dipping night..." Clifton lowers his voice. "I have a feeling you organized that too."

"It was so hot in those cabins," Mercedes says, glancing at me. "I was just cooling off with a midnight swim, and my suit was still drying from earlier that day. How was I to know everyone would follow little ole me?"

Clifton is about to make a comment, but I stand and put my napkin over my plate.

"I hope you've enjoyed your evening," I say to Clifton.

Clifton takes the hint and begins to rise, but Mercedes grabs his hand and holds it. "Sit, Clifton. We haven't even had dessert. Besides, this is the most fun I've had in forever."

"Well," Clifton looks at me. "If Judge says—"

"Pfft. Judge will be fine. He's much older than us," she says conspiratorially to him but loud enough for me to hear. "He needs to get his rest what with his important work. You go on to bed, Judge. I'll make sure Clifton is… entertained."

When I take a step toward their end of the table, I'm not sure if I'm going to grab her by the hair and haul her to her feet or take him by the collar and kick him out, but I do neither as Clifton pulls his hand free.

"I'd better go anyway. I have an early day tomorrow." Clifton stumbles over his words, nearly knocking his chair over to put distance between himself and Mercedes.

"That's a good idea," I say. Mercedes makes to rise, but I set a heavy hand on her shoulder to stop her. "I'll walk you out."

"I'll come too," Mercedes tries again to stand, and I squeeze, then lean down until my mouth is beside her ear.

"You'll go upstairs and wait for me to come up. I'll deal with you then."

18

JUDGE

It takes all I have not to shove Clifton out the door. Truth be told, I feel sorry for him. Mercedes and I both used him tonight.

But as soon as he's gone, I take the stairs two at a time, and on the landing, I watch Mercedes. She's only halfway down the hall because she must have been eavesdropping. Her hands are fists as she walks angrily to my room.

"You don't want me, but you won't let me go, either," she accuses as soon as I'm inside and I've closed the door behind me. "You play with me like I'm a fucking yo-yo, and I'm done!" She stalks into my closet to start pulling out her clothes and tossing them onto the floor in her rage.

I grab her arm and spin her to face me. "What the fuck was that?"

She tugs free and shoves me with both hands.

Sadly for her, she can't budge me, so she takes a step back to put space between us.

"That was me trying to get a husband. Remember that little thing, Judge? All good Society girls need a man to manage them. You've made it very fucking clear that you don't want me. Like I told you the last time we talked fucking weeks ago before you did what you do best and disappeared. Again."

"You think your behavior was appropriate tonight?"

"What? I can't flirt with a man I'm attracted to?"

"You're not attracted to him!"

"No? How do you know?"

"Because I know your type."

"And what's that? Big giant bully who likes to humiliate me again and again and fucking again?"

"I keep you away for your own good."

"You just keep telling yourself you're doing this all for me. You just wasted my chance."

"What chance? You'd really marry that man? That boy? He's at the bottom of his class. His family isn't exactly swimming in money. What do you think he wants out of a marriage with you?"

"Unlike you, I don't fool myself, Judge. I know I won't marry for love—"

"Love?"

"Yes. Love. And I'm sure that sounds pathetic to someone like you. And really, how can I blame you? I have a history. Does Mercedes De La Rosa even have the capacity to love? I'm a fucking ice queen without feelings. Isn't that what they all say? I had a chance tonight!"

"That's not what I meant."

"And don't forget you're the one who invited him."

"After I saw your text—"

"You what?" She stops, her eyes narrowing to slits, fists clenched so tight her whole body is shaking. "You fucking asshole!" She flies at me, hands like claws.

I catch her when she hurls her weight into me.

"This is what I mean! You run too hot. The fire inside you would be wasted on a man like that," I tell her as she draws one arm back to slap me. I take the sting of it as she rages, all nails and fists and fury. I spin her, throw her onto the bed and grip her wrists at her lower back. She wriggles to get free. "You think you'd be happy with someone like Clifton fucking Phillips?" Switching her wrists into one hand, I take hold of the top of her dress with the other and rip it straight down the middle. "You think you could ever be satisfied with someone like that? You think he's your match in any way?" I tear away the string that barely qualifies as panties.

"What's the matter, Judge?" She twists her neck to look back at me. "You don't want someone touching what's yours? Temporarily, I might add. Can't stomach the idea of me getting off on someone else's dick? Get the fuck off me!"

I look around, half mad with rage and jealousy and God knows what, and see her lotion on the nightstand. I reach for it, keeping hold of her wrists as I do, and flip the top open.

"What the fuck are you doing?" she asks when I squeeze a healthy amount onto her lower back.

I undo my belt and slacks, pushing them down only as far as I have to in order to free my cock. Scooping up the lotion, I smear it over my dick, then lift her by her hips, digging my fingers into tender flesh to keep her in position. I push her knees apart with my own and look down at her.

"I'm giving you what you want," I tell her.

"At least be honest with yourself. You want it, too. You want me. The difference between us is that you can't stand yourself for it."

I don't answer her. Instead, I brush my thumb over her tight hole. She stiffens. But it's when I push against it that her eyes go wide and she realizes how I intend to take her.

"Judge!"

I meet those eyes with a grin. "Try to relax." I release her wrists and grip her ass cheeks, splaying her wide. Fuck, she's so beautiful. "It'll be easier for you to take me in your tight little ass if you relax." I shift my gaze back to hers. "And you will take me. All of me."

"Judge, you can't—"

She sucks in a breath as I guide the head of my cock into her. She's tight. Too tight.

"You'll tear me in two!" She fists the sheets. I think she's trying to crawl away.

I slap her hip. "I said relax." I push in, resisting the urge to thrust into her, groaning at the tight squeeze of her passage on my cock.

"Oh, God. I can't. I…"

I slip one hand around to her clit as I push deeper, watching my cock disappear inside her.

"You're going to kill me," she manages more quietly.

Leaning over her, I bite the curve of her shoulder. "I'm going to make you come hard, little monster." With that, I thrust into her, unable to hold back any longer.

She cries out, and I have to haul her hips back up. I draw out and thrust again.

"Please!"

"Shh. You can take me, Mercedes." I make myself still and rub her clit, savoring the feel of her.

She lays her cheek down with a moan in a sort of surrender.

"Good. That's good. Just relax."

Her slickness coats my fingers, and all I can

think is I need to come inside her. I need it. She whimpers, and I lay my body over hers and kiss her temple, holding her tight to me. Her eyes go glassy. I kiss her cheek, her eyelid, the corner of her mouth as I feel her from the inside, owning her.

"It feels... I'm going to come," she manages, her breath catching. Gripping a handful of hair, I haul her up so her back is to my front. She closes her hands over my thighs, murmuring words I can't make out as I kiss her, continuing to push into her.

"Do you feel what happens to me when I'm inside you? What you fucking do to me? The thought of that man touching you, of any man touching you, makes me fucking crazy."

Her gaze flicks to mine, and she licks her lips.

"But you like hearing that, don't you, little monster?" I close my teeth over the pulse at her neck, then push her back down onto her hands and knees and watch myself fuck her, taking this other piece of her.

She whimpers, then closes her eyes and begins to meet my thrusts. It's the hottest thing I've ever seen. Sweat from my forehead drips onto her back, and I want to fuck her like this all night. Because it's not enough. It'll never be enough. I'll never get enough of her. And when she fists the sheets and shudders around me, the tremors are too much, and I come too, pinning her with my weight and holding her tight as I empty inside her.

When it's over and we've stilled, both of us panting, I push the hair from her face and kiss her temple, which is damp with sweat. I listen to her breathe, lifting some of my weight off her.

She mutters my name, the sound sad. A little broken.

I pull out slowly, and she trembles when I lift off altogether. I put the blanket over her and go into the bathroom to wash up and return with a warm washcloth. I sit on the bed beside her and clean her. She's quiet and still.

"I lose control with you, Mercedes. Every time. I know it's wrong, but I can't fucking give you up. I just don't know how to keep you."

She turns to look up at me with wet eyes and sits up drawing her knees to her chest, gaze drifting away from me as her forehead creases. I try to brush her hair back from her face, but she pushes my hand away before shifting her gaze to me.

"You're right," she says, and something in the way she sounds makes my chest tighten. "I wouldn't ever be happy with someone like Clifton Phillips. I know that. But I can't do this anymore either. It's too much, and I can't."

I open my mouth to answer but my phone

rings. We both turn to look at it, and Mercedes's breath catches when she sees it's Santiago.

"Mercedes—" I start, but she shakes her head, grabs the phone, and answers it.

"Santi? Is the baby okay? Is Ivy?"

I hear the rumble of his voice, but I can't make out the words.

Mercedes presses a fist to her mouth, tears suddenly pouring from her eyes. I take the phone from her.

"Santiago? What is it? What's happened?"

"She woke up. Ivy woke up."

19

MERCEDES

"How are they?" I ask.

I hear shuffling on the other end of the line before Santi answers distractedly. "They are both doing well. Keeping me busy. Ivy's rehabilitation is progressing, and she's improving every day."

"That's so great to hear," I tell him.

The silence on the other end of the line makes me think Santiago doesn't believe me, and he never will.

"When can I come meet my niece?"

"I don't know yet." His tone takes on a hard edge.

I swallow, and it feels like there's glass lodged in my throat. I get why he's so protective of them. They've been through hell, and part of that is my fault. He's making it clear it's not a matter of choosing sides anymore. His loyalty lies with his wife and daughter, and they are his family now.

It fucking hurts, but I get it. Oddly enough, I get it more than he could probably understand at this moment, with a child of my own growing inside me. I will always choose this child above anyone or anything.

"Santi—" My voice fractures, and I try to hold it together. "I know things have been tense. I know I've been awful. And you probably won't believe me when I tell you I regret it, but I do. I want to be a part of your lives. I want to come see you and Ivy, and I want to meet Elena."

"Mercedes." He sighs, shuffling the phone again as Elena cries in the background. "I don't know yet."

"Please," I beg. "I need to see you. It's important."

I don't tell him that I want to have a conversation with him about releasing me from Judge's care because he'll think that's my only motivation, and that's not true. I really do want to meet my niece.

"Let me think about it," he says.

The crying gets louder, and I can just imagine him picking up his baby daughter, and my heart squeezes at the thought of it. Not only because I'm missing it, but because I never thought I'd see Santi as a father. I never thought I'd see him love the woman he once talked about killing in cold blood. Yet he is.

If I believed in hope, this might have given me some. Because if Santi can fall for his enemy, then surely, Judge can fall for someone he admits he can't let go of. But I can't go down that path again. Not now. Maybe not ever. Judge has proven over and over again that the only thing he's capable of is breaking hearts. Regardless, what he wants doesn't matter now. It can't. Not with the decision I made when I failed to swallow what he thought was a mistake.

"Please let me know," I whisper into the phone. "I really do want to come see her."

"I'll let you know," Santi answers, distracted by his current situation. "I have to go."

"Okay, I'll speak to you soon then?"

"Yeah," he says, and before I can draw another breath, he disconnects the call.

I sit on the bed, staring at the wall. Judge is gone, God knows where, but that would require him sharing his life with me. Since our spat, he's been wavering between putting distance between us and then acting as if nothing ever happened when he comes to lie beside me at night. Sometimes, his determination wins, and other times, it fails him. When he reaches out to touch me on those nights it fails, I let him. I let him because as much as it hurts, I want it. I know I won't be able to have it forever, so I take it while I can. I take it before our time is up indefinitely, and he'll never want to touch me again.

"Mercedes." Lois knocks on my door, drawing my attention to her. "Solana is here. Would you like me to send her up?"

"Oh, yes, thank you. That would be perfect."

She nods and retreats, and I use the few moments I have to check my makeup and try to cover up the dark circles beneath my eyes with some powder. But it doesn't work, and that much is obvious as soon as Solana enters and sees me.

"You look tired." She frowns.

"That's because I am." I laugh hollowly. "I hear that's a side effect of a tiny life force growing inside you."

She walks over and gives me a tight squeeze before pulling her messenger bag off her shoulder and setting it on the bed.

"Well, I brought what you needed." She hands me the pregnancy test and then retrieves a bottle with her shop label on it. "And these aren't really calming tablets. I just put the label over some prenatal vitamins."

"You think of everything." I offer her a watery smile.

"I know." She returns my smile, but her concern is evident. "Are you okay?"

"I will be," I answer. "It's just... a lot."

"Well, let's take things one step at a time, shall we?" She grabs my hand and tugs me toward the bathroom. "First step, peeing on a stick."

Five minutes later, I'm sitting on the edge of the porcelain tub while Solana peers down at the stick resting on the sink.

"Good news or bad news?" she asks.

"Both," I answer in amusement.

"The good news is I'm going to be the best freaking godmother this kid could ever ask for," she says proudly. "And the bad news is anyone who ever even thinks of hurting him or her will have to reckon with me."

I can't help laughing even as a few tears spill free, and I press my hands to my belly. I already knew it was real, but this confirms it.

"She's not lying," I whisper to the baby growing inside me. "But I think you'll love your crazy aunt Solana."

"Damn straight they will." Solana comes to kneel before me, wiping my tears away. "It's going to be okay. You know that, don't you? You've got me, and you've got Georgie, no matter what, always. We are your motherfucking family."

"I know you are." I pull her in for a hug, and she squeezes me for a long time.

Finally, after a prolonged pause to let the official news sink in, she comes to sit beside me on the tub. "Are you going to tell him?"

"No." I shake my head quickly. "He doesn't want kids. This was my decision, not his. He won't be happy when he finds out, but I want nothing from him. I won't ask him for anything. I just want this baby, and he can go on with his life, forgetting either of us exist."

By the tense silence next to me, I probably shouldn't have been so honest. Because Solana really will cut a motherfucker for me or anyone else she loves. I know and love this about her. But I don't want her protection. I just want her friendship. I want to tell her everything about my life because I'm so fucking tired of shouldering it on my own.

"You want me to poison him?" she asks, her voice dead serious.

Again, I can't help laughing. "No. But thank you." I turn to her and take her hands in mine. "What I want is to tell you about my world, Solana. I think it's time I finally did."

She releases a breath, nods, and listens to all of it. Every single secret that spills from my lips.

AFTER SPILLING ALL the details of my life to Solana, she and Georgie have been making frequent visits. As in, almost every day. I was nervous about telling Georgie my secrets too, given that he's even more protective than Solana, but I didn't want to keep lying to them or giving them half-truths. So after getting him up to speed on all need-to-know things related to The Society and my pregnancy, everything is out in the open. I thought I'd be more relieved, but I'm questioning if I did the right thing because they're both convinced I might just up and disappear at any moment in this crazy world they still don't fully understand.

I've tried to quell their fears, but honestly, they aren't too far off the mark. I was raised in this world, so I never really realized before how insane it sounds to normal people on the outside. People do disappear in The Society. They get murdered and tossed into Tribunal prison cells that nobody knows anything about. They get poisoned, betrayed, and double-crossed, and that's just a small taste of any given week. But even so, I had no reason to be concerned for my safety. That was until I noticed Georgie and Solana exchanging looks like they know something I don't. When I demanded they tell me, they finally relented.

Apparently, Judge is fielding some sort of threat. Whoever tainted the beignets is after me, and they also went to Solana's house in an effort to track me down. It's a realization that scares me because she doesn't have the same level of protection I do. But she assured me Judge has people watching her, which is strange. And it pisses me the hell off that he's been hiding this from me.

He mentioned something about Abel, but since Abel has already been captured and we're attending his trial today, I know that can't be the case. If it was him, Judge wouldn't still have guards following Solana or lurking in the yard outside. It has to be someone else, though I know there's no point in asking him. I can see that today when he comes into the room while I'm getting ready.

He watches my reflection in the mirror as I apply my lipstick and smooth my hair back. His annoyance is obvious, and I don't have to wonder why. He's taken notice Solana and Georgie have been visiting far more often, and I've been waiting for him to say something about it.

"Why aren't you wearing your necklace?" His narrowed gaze roams over the empty space around my collarbones.

I meet his gaze in the reflection. "It wouldn't do to have Santi see it and wonder where it's from, now, would it?"

He grunts in response, dragging a hand over his face as if it never occurred to him. I roll my eyes but try not to let him sour my mood. Santiago finally agreed to let me come to the manor before we all leave for the trial, and I have no intentions of anything raining on that parade. Not today. Judge, however, has other plans.

"Are you going to tell me why your friends have been over almost every day?" He brushes my hair over my shoulder, his fingers settling onto the nape of my neck.

"I know this is a foreign concept to you, but my friends actually like me," I tell him. "They enjoy visiting with me."

"And that's why they suddenly seem to be glaring at me every time I cross paths with them?" His thumb skates over the empty space reserved for my future husband, and I shiver.

"Perhaps you need to take some charm lessons," I suggest. "Solana and Georgie love everyone. You must be the exception."

He doesn't respond, but I can feel his gaze burning into me as I apply another smidge of powder I don't really need.

"Perhaps until they can learn to be polite, I need to limit their visits to the house."

I turn around to glare at him. "Do you get off on making me miserable? Is that it?"

His jaw muscle ticks, and he shakes his head. "I don't want you to be miserable, Mercedes. Quite the opposite."

"You have a funny way of showing it." I slam the compact on the vanity table shut and stand, shrugging his hand off my neck.

I try to escape into the bathroom, but he grabs me by the wrist and tugs me back to him. I'm expecting another argument, but when I look up into his eyes, there's a softness I almost wish he wouldn't show me. It makes it so much harder to maintain my emotions around him.

"Today will be difficult enough." He strokes along my jaw, his eyes moving over my features as if he's trying to memorize them. "Let's call a cease-fire for now."

I release a staggering breath, and he leans in, surprising me with a kiss. It's different from his other kisses. He's not branding me with his intensity like I'm used to. This is something softer. Something he's taking simply because he feels like it at the moment. And goddammit if that doesn't feel like another dagger to my heart.

"Don't be nice to me," I beg him as he releases me. "Please."

"Why?" His brows crease together.

I square my shoulders and shake my head. "Because. I just... don't want you to."

The vein in his neck pulses an angry beat, but he doesn't argue. At least for now.

"We're going to be late." He heads to the door, leaving me to follow him. "Let's go."

20

MERCEDES

I'm a wreck of nerves when I squeeze Santi in the first hug I've given him in so long. A weird sound strangles my throat, betraying my emotions, and he pats me awkwardly in an attempt to comfort me.

"I've missed you so much," I croak.

"I know," he answers. "I've missed you too."

I hold him at arm's length, examining him. He's still the same scarred man who crawled from the ashes of the wreckage that imploded our lives. But something about the way he carries himself is lighter. Though his eyes are no less intense.

"You look different," I observe.

He shifts. "A lot has changed."

I force a stiff nod, understanding tension still lingers between us as my eyes roam to Ivy. She's sitting across the room with Elena, and I force a smile, hoping she can see it's genuine.

"When can I meet my niece?"

"I'm not sure if that's such a good idea," Santi answers.

I can feel my chest caving in, pain lancing through me, and Judge seems to sense it too as his hand settles on my back. At least, that's until my brother notices it, and the warmth of Judge's comfort falls away.

"Mercedes will behave," he assures Santiago in an authoritative tone. "And she would very much like to meet her niece if you'll let her."

Santi's gaze moves to Ivy, and mine does too. It's in her hands, and I understand that. I'd also understand if she said no, but she's a better person than I am. She rises from her chair, rocking Elena in her arms as she approaches, but Santi intercepts her halfway. His hand settles on her hip as he leans down to whisper in her ear.

I wait quietly while she answers him, her eyes on mine. I feel like I'm frozen in place as she finally approaches me, and it's hard to know what to do. I want to thank her, but I don't know how.

"Ivy," I choke out a clumsy greeting. "I'm happy to see you are recovering well."

"Is that so?" Ivy returns, her voice not completely absent of the ice I deserve.

"Yes." I dip my head, trying not to let myself get

crazy emotional. "I know I can be a spoiled, jealous bitch sometimes, okay? I can admit, I've done some things I'm not proud of, and for that I am sorry. But you obviously make my brother very happy, and I see that you're here to stay, so I would like to try to get to know you. If you'll let me."

Ivy seems surprised by my admission, but her face softens, and I want to believe this bridge hasn't burned entirely.

"I think that would be beneficial for all of us," she says, shifting Elena so I can see her. "This is your niece, Elena Frances De La Rosa."

"She's beautiful." I bring a trembling hand to my lips, tears filling my eyes. "Can I hold her for a minute?"

Ivy looks at Santi, and he nods back at her. "That's up to you."

She considers it for a moment and then helps me take the small bundle into my arms. I stare down at her in awe, marveling at her innocence. That sweet baby smell. My heart floods with warmth, and I know everyone can see it. The tension radiating from Judge beside me is palpable, but I only have eyes for my beautiful niece. She's truly amazing, and more than anything, I know I want and need to be a part of her life.

"One day, you will have your own," Santi murmurs approvingly.

He couldn't have any idea how much his words

terrify me. I know he's thinking way into the future, but at some point, he will learn it really isn't that far off at all. Hoping they can't see the flush crawling down my neck, I crack a joke.

"Maybe I'll have a whole brood of them. Ten little monsters just like me."

Santi snorts at the notion. "What do you think of that idea, Judge?"

Against all rational sense, my eyes snap up to his. "Yes, Judge. What do you think of that?"

He narrows his eyes, but it doesn't hide his obvious displeasure at the thought. "She can do what she likes... once she's proven herself capable."

His answer feels as visceral as a slap to the face, and I wish more than anything I hadn't heard it, even if I already knew deep down that's how he feels. It serves as a reminder that I can't let him in again. Every touch, every soft word... they are all designed to lure me back to him, but if he knew the truth, he wouldn't want anything to do with me. It's up to me now to leave him before he can make that decision. Before he can serve me the ultimate and most painful rejection of my life.

My baby deserves more than that, and I will never let our child know anything but love. I might not know much of it myself, but I will learn, and it will pour out of me so fiercely, I pray he or she will never feel his absence in the way I surely will.

"A conversation for another time," Santi says, sensing the tension I wish wasn't so obvious.

"Thank you for letting me meet her." I hand Elena back to Ivy. "I suppose we should probably get going now."

Santi agrees, and they inform us they'll meet us outside. I don't wait for Judge, but I can feel him watching me as we venture out onto the steps of the manor. It's strange how this place that was once my home no longer feels that way. I'd been so jealous of Ivy coming here, taking over everything, and pushing me out of the house I grew up in. But as I stand here, silent, my eyes moving over the beautiful architecture, it feels like a chapter of my life I never want to revisit again.

I understand now that home is not just a place but a feeling. And I'm going to make a home for my baby and me. Somewhere safe. Somewhere violence has never touched. And I will do it without the man beside me, no matter how much my heart aches.

It's funny how time changes one's perspective. For years, I have waited for the Morenos to be brought to justice. In one horrific night, I lost my father and brother Leandro to the explosion linked back to this family. Santiago barely survived himself, crawling from the flames, his flesh forever marred by the events. I clung to the hope that he would live, begging God and every other deity that might exist to save him as he faced a brutal recovery that most would not be strong enough to endure. And then came the news that our mother died—a result of her grief, no doubt.

What was left behind in the wreckage of those months were a brother and sister who'd had everyone they'd ever loved ripped away. We vowed revenge. We plotted it, and we relished it with a fervency that burned the blood in my veins, twisting and gnarling me into something I didn't particularly like.

We wanted every Moreno to pay. It didn't matter the cost. It didn't matter their involvement. They all needed to suffer as we had. It was the only thing that made sense. At least, that was what I thought until Santiago fell in love, and the truth began to slowly unfurl.

I now understand who was responsible, and as I sit through Abel Moreno's trial, listening to all of his sins and misdeeds, two things become evident. The first is that I was becoming just like him. So twisted up in my grief and desire for revenge, I couldn't see wrong from right. And the second is that I just don't have the energy to carry that burden of hate anymore. All it's managed to do is poison me, and for the sake of my sanity, I understand I have to let it go. But I also understand that, on some level, I already have. Because there are bigger things on the horizon now. I have a life waiting for me, and I still don't entirely know what that life will look like, but I know I don't want it to be tainted by these memories.

Yet as I listen to The Tribunal sentence Abel to death, I can't help the uneasy feeling that settles over me when his eyes move to mine. Today, I will wash my hands of him and never want to think of him again. But I can't help wondering if he has concessions for that. I don't doubt he would have revealed my plan to The Tribunal in an effort to save his own skin. He probably told them of my involvement in trying to lure Santiago to adultery, which inadvertently got him poisoned. That was never my intention, nor my plan, but Abel schemed and made it so.

Regardless, I know it doesn't matter how it happened. The fact is it did, and I could still be held responsible for it. By the evil glint in his eyes right now, I don't doubt that's exactly what he's trying to tell me.

A shudder moves over me, and then the room falls to silence as the final word is passed down, and we are all told to adjourn to the courtyard. I move in a daze, Judge pressing his hand against my lower back in a silent show of support. The night sky is black when we step out and gather before the gallows. We've been here for many hours, and it's late now. The normal raucous crowd surrounding the IVI compound is absent, and instead, there are only soft murmurs that fall into silence as the process begins.

Every Society member who has been wronged by Abel is given an opportunity to speak, and there are many of them. It goes on for what feels like hours, and another wave of emotion crashes over me, exhaustion mingling with finality. I haven't witnessed a Society execution before. This will be the first I've attended, and hopefully my last. They do happen, though not commonly. It takes a lot for The Tribunal to hand down a sentence such as this. I only know I will be grateful when it's over. Despite my resolve to keep my emotions in check, my eyes sting with unshed tears as the weight of it all settles over me. This is it. The culmination of all my grief—all the tension between my brother and me, the painful memories, and the past we didn't know we'd ever be able to leave behind. After today, there's no doubt in my mind we will. We'll have no choice.

"It's our turn," I whisper to Santi.

He nods, and Judge releases me reluctantly. Together, Santi and I walk up to the platform, standing before the smug asshole who sent our lives spiraling into chaos and misery. Santi holds me close, and I stare at the face of the man I swear

I will never allow to haunt us again. He refuses to meet my eyes, refuses to act as if he cares about the fate about to befall him.

Santi speaks to him first, low and vicious, his words unfaltering. I only catch a few of them, lost in my own thoughts, unable to take my eyes off the man who will cease to exist after this day. I consider my own words to him, if there is anything I need to say, but I realize as my brother finishes, Abel Moreno neither deserves nor cares about my thoughts or feelings. Santi seems to sense this, and when he finishes, he turns us both to take our leave until I halt him.

I pull away from him, stepping close to Abel as I steel all my strength, and he finally dares another smug glance at my face. No, I certainly have no speech for him. But I do have something. I hurl my disgust and venom from my lips, spitting into his face.

"I will do the same to your grave," I tell him with a smile. "Enjoy your death, you miserable bastard. You've earned it."

21

JUDGE

Capital punishment is legal in the state of Louisiana, but no one has been put to death in over a decade. The last execution carried out by the state was voluntary.

The Tribunal is a different matter. Abel Moreno's execution was one of two that took place in my lifetime. My personal beliefs don't matter when it comes to my courtroom, but I am grateful never to have had to sentence someone to such a fate.

Abel Moreno's death was a necessary one. Tonight, a chapter was closed. But if anyone thought they'd be dancing on the bastard's grave, they're mistaken. Death is still death. A human life snuffed out. And an execution is not a peaceful end.

Mercedes has been in the shower for almost

half an hour when I ignore her call to go away and unlock the bathroom door to enter. Steam makes it almost impossible to see, and I'm pretty sure she's in there to muffle the sounds of her crying.

"You're going to turn into a raisin." Rolling up my shirtsleeve, I open the glass door and switch off the water.

"I wasn't done."

"Come on, little monster." I reach for a towel, unfold it, and hold it up for her to step into. She looks different. She hasn't lost weight exactly. Her breasts appear plumper but there's almost a gauntness to the rest of her. Although perhaps it's the way she's standing with her shoulders slumped, toes turned in, making her look smaller.

She steps into the towel. I wrap it around her shoulders, then lift her in my arms. She's surprised but doesn't resist as I carry her into the bedroom, where I sit on the bed with her on my lap.

"Your clothes are going to get wet."

"They'll dry."

There's something about this moment that I want to hold on to. A softness in her yielding to me as she rests her head against my chest and sighs.

"It's all right to be upset."

She shrugs a shoulder.

"A man died tonight. And you witnessed it." Although she didn't see him hang. The women who were permitted to be present during the execution were made to turn away before the lever was pulled.

"He was horrible. He destroyed my family."

"I know. But your family is rebuilding itself. Santiago is happy. He has a wife he loves and a child."

She sniffles.

"And you will be happy too. I promise."

She turns her gaze to mine. "How can you make a promise like that? It's not realistic. There's no way you can keep it."

I feel myself tense. I know what she wants. What she *still* wants. And there's a part of me that wants it too. To keep her. But it's true what I said. I don't know how.

Her comment from earlier comes to mind. It's been repeating ever since she said it. *Don't be nice to me.* And each time I remember how she sounded when she said it, something tightens inside me, making my chest constrict. Making it hard to breathe.

The Mercedes who first came here is a distant memory to the woman in my arms now. There are glimpses of her, to be sure, but less and less. She has grown. She is learning from her mistakes. She wants to make amends. I know what it took for her to apologize to Ivy. To ask to be included in their lives. The Mercedes of before would not have done that. Not even close.

What I don't like is the sadness. This shadow swells ever bigger, taking up more space both inside and outside of her. And I know I am to blame for it.

Don't be nice to me.

Because it would be easier if she hated me. And she may in some way. I've broken something inside her, just as she has me.

What a mess I've made. It's easier when we fight. When we fuck.

Mercedes shivers, and I stand her up. She lets me dry her, her eyes on my face. My shirt is soaked, so I take it off and toss it aside. From beneath her pillow—when did it become hers, when did she get a side of my bed—I retrieve her pajama set. Silk shorts and a matching tank top.

"Theron did this the night you saved me from him," she says, and for a moment, I am confused, but then she touches the small scar high on my cheekbone.

"I did worse to him." I look her over, see the tiny triangle of dark hair she's let grow between her legs. I like it. I like to run my fingers through it.

"Judge?"

When I drag my gaze to her eyes, she's watching me. I set the pajamas aside. I cup her face, my thumb brushing her lips, knuckles sliding over one taut nipple as I drop to my knees before her. She swallows, weaves the fingers of one hand in my hair when I turn my attention to that small patch of soft hair and open her. I inhale her clean scent, then run the pad of my tongue over her. She shudders, and her fingers tighten. I lick again, hearing her moan when I nip at her clit. When I lift one of her legs over my shoulder, she holds on to me for balance.

I take her slowly. I rarely make love to her. We normally fuck. We fuck hard and rough, but this is different. Tonight, she needs soft. And I give it to her first with my tongue, devouring her, her taste and her scent an aphrodisiac. And when she comes, her standing leg buckles, and she leans into me, moaning, her grip on me so tight it's like she's pulling my hair out.

When she goes limp, I lift her thigh from my shoulder and stand, carrying her to the bed to lay her on her back. I climb between her legs and kiss her with my mouth still wet from her. Her hands come around my waist, one settling on the scar on my back as she kisses me, a deep, slow kiss. Perhaps it's not only her who needs soft right now.

I slide easily into her, thinking the impossible as I do. Three little words that I can never utter. The only ones I can think. I can feel. It would be so natural. So easy to say them. But the consequence would be fatal.

So I make love to her without ever saying the words. We watch each other without speaking. We kiss, never taking our eyes from one another. Tonight is not even about reaching a climax. It's her clinging to me and me clinging to her and possibly being the closest we've ever been. As close as two human beings can get without burrowing beneath the other's skin.

I pull out before I come. I've been careful about that, although I know I should use a condom. I just can't with her. I need her heat. Skin on skin, I need to feel her.

When it's over, we lie together, her on her back, me on my side holding her. Her fingers play over the scar on my back.

"Theron," I say.

She looks at me, and it takes her a minute to understand.

"At his twenty-fifth birthday celebration."

Her eyes grow more alert, and she turns toward me, fingers coming to my face.

"It's when the Montgomery men receive the first installment of our inheritance."

She doesn't speak, just waits.

"I'm going to tell you a secret, Mercedes. Something I've never told anyone." I brush a strand of hair that's fallen across her forehead, and for a long time, I just look at her. It's so long she must think I've changed my mind and gives me an out.

"You don't have to tell me." She sounds disappointed but unsurprised.

"I want to."

She waits.

"We had a celebration on his birthday. I already knew the truth by then, but I didn't know what my grandfather had planned. He was a cruel man. I think that was the day I realized how cruel even after everything I had seen."

Mercedes curls into my side. I draw the blanket up to cover her when she shivers, and although I don't look at her, I can see her in my periphery. She's watching me intently.

"After the meal came time for cake, and before that, Theron would sign the papers. I had done it the previous year, almost to the day. Theron was the only one at that table who was truly excited that evening. Almost buoyant. Maybe my mother and I both suspected my grandfather's plan. His strange glee at dinner gave him away.

"Once dinner was cleared, my grandfather laid out the papers and uncapped the pen. He signed his name to the forms and then stood back and watched my brother. Watched him as he read the pages and understood what was happening."

"What was it?" she asks after too long a pause.

I look down at her eager, open face. "He isn't a Montgomery. Not by blood."

"What?"

"My parents' match was not a love match, but so few are. She had an affair. And Theron was the product of that affair. My grandfather learned the truth when Theron was fifteen. Thankfully he was away at school when all hell broke loose within the walls of the Montgomery estate."

"What did he do?"

How much do I want to tell her? I've come this far. *We've* come this far.

"He punished my mother." A long silence draws out, and I have to force the next words. My confession. "And I stood witness."

"What do you mean?" she asks with a tremor in her voice. I'm sure she is remembering the punishment room.

"He made her strip. Made my mother strip naked in front of me. And he whipped her raw." Mercedes's hand flies to her mouth. "The scars go from the tops of her shoulders to the backs of her ankles."

"Oh, my God."

"I stood and watched. I listened to her scream and sob and beg him to stop."

"Jesus."

"And I did nothing."

"Judge, you were sixteen years old. A boy."

I shake my head. "He made her believe if she paid the price, he would accept Theron. Someone had to be punished, after all. She sacrificed herself for her son."

"Oh…"

"She was noble once. He broke her of that, though."

She straddles me and cups my face with both hands. It takes my eyes time to focus on her because I think I was gone for a minute there. Back in that room. Back to the sight of my mother enduring my grandfather's wrath.

"And when Theron learned the truth the night of his birthday, the night he should have celebrated a sort of coming of age, he changed. It happened before my eyes. He asked me if I'd known, and I couldn't answer him. I didn't need to, though he saw it on my face. I still remember how he hugged me. And how the knife felt sliding easily into my back. The pain of it. And then not much else."

"Jesus Christ."

She hugs me, and I find myself clinging to her, her weight slight on top of me, but her presence solid and warm and so fucking necessary. And I know without a doubt that what I feel for her I have never felt for anyone before. Ever.

"It's not your fault. You know that, right? Please tell me you know that."

I cup her face, feeling myself harden even now, even with what I just exposed. "I do, my sweet little monster. But I also know my temper. It matches his. Surpasses it."

"What are you talking about?"

"Carlisle. His rage skipped a generation and landed heavy in the next."

"That's what you think?"

"That's what I know."

"And the reason you won't marry. Because you think you'll repeat history. You think you'll hurt me like he did her."

I try to push her off and get up because this isn't where I wanted to end up when I started this story. But she doesn't let me go. She sets her thighs firmly on either side of me, presses her soft breasts into my chest, and kisses me.

"You're an idiot, Lawson Montgomery," she says, kissing me again as she sheathes herself on me.

"And you are going to be the death of me," I tell her, wrapping my arms around her and pushing deep into her. I shift my hands to her hips to move her over me all the while kissing and biting her lips as she kisses and bites mine, her moans growing louder as my thrusts become more urgent. And when I try to pull out, she grips me tight, the muscles of her legs pressing into me, and even though I could flip her off, do the less wrong thing and not come inside her again, I don't. I hold on tight and listen to her pant my name as I come inside her.

22

JUDGE

The next few weeks pass in a lasting cease-fire. We are tender toward one another. We make love. We lie together in bed, Mercedes curling into my side. I hold her and wonder how I will ever sleep in this bed when she is no longer in it.

But I try not to think about that. I want to hold on to this tenderness a while longer. Already the end is near. I received a call from Hildebrand. Well, a summons. Not me, but Mercedes, although I haven't told her about it yet. I have put him off, but not for very much longer. I have a feeling I know what he'll require of her because she won't walk away from her role in Santiago's poisoning scot-free. No one does, not from The Tribunal.

But I'm not ready to burst this bubble we're squatting in just yet. Two interlopers. Almost happy. Almost because we both know the end is coming. These are stolen moments.

She calls her brother and Ivy almost daily. She asks to listen to the baby coo. Asks questions about how Ivy is doing. How the baby is doing. What it's like to feed her. To hold her. She has sent countless presents for the baby. Two full wardrobes and enough toys to stock a shop. But she has only seen Elena three more times since she first met her.

I disagree with Santiago on this. He should give her more of himself, more of them. But he keeps her on the outside, and she is abundantly clear of the fact.

Mercedes is napping before dinner, and I don't tell her when I pay a visit to the De La Rosa Manor. Calling would be easier, but I can't risk her overhearing my conversation with her brother. Santiago and I settle into his office after a brief visit with Ivy. She's still skittish around me and won't be alone in a room with me. I understand even though I try to be as innocuous as possible.

"She will learn you are no threat to her," Santiago tells me as he pours us each a scotch.

"I understand. It will take time."

"I heard the night with Clifton Phillips was not quite a success." He says it with a small grin.

"I didn't think it would be. He's a child. Neither capable nor worthy of Mercedes."

"You've gotten to know my sister well. Better than I, perhaps."

"She is different, Santiago. You should get to know this true Mercedes."

"In time. The courtesan's brother... has there been any word on his location?"

"No. Nothing. He's all but disappeared. I have the houses of both Solana and Georgie under surveillance as well as their shops. My home is secure. No one will get to Mercedes there. And I, or should I say she, hasn't received any more threatening texts on the old phone."

"Which is worrying."

"Agree."

"And she still doesn't know about him?"

"I haven't told her. I thought it would be best."

"And this Ezra Moore, you trust him?"

"I do. He'll find him. He has resources and will use them."

"Good."

"How is your brother?" I told Santiago about the attack on him but left out the part where Mercedes was concerned.

"Recovering, according to Ezra. I will pay him a visit soon."

"And he'll return to the house?"

"We'll see."

"What happened between you two? There's bad blood. I can smell it, Judge."

"It's hardly worth discussing. Not when Hildebrand is looking for blood himself."

"Fucking asshole."

"I've put him off for a few weeks, but I will pay him a visit once I leave here. I want to talk to him privately. See what he knows and if I can influence the consequence." Consequence. Mercedes's punishment. Hildebrand, much like my grandfather, is a stickler for the rules. A crime must be punished. Balance restored.

"What will he demand?" In Santiago's voice, I hear his concern for his sister. She'd be comforted to know it.

"I don't know," I tell Santiago. "She was deceived. I can't imagine more than community service."

"Which will humiliate her."

"But it's better than a harsher sentence." Payment in flesh.

Santiago nods because he understands. "She doesn't go into The Tribunal building without you or me at her side. She doesn't set foot on the compound without us. I don't trust him not to take her into custody."

"We're on the same page. I will protect your sister, Santiago. I won't let them lay a finger on her."

His head tilts just a little, such an infinitesimal movement it's almost imperceptible.

I clear my throat. "As your sister, I care for her, much the same as I do you, Ivy, and your child. I wouldn't let anything happen to any of you if I could help it."

"Thank you, Judge."

My phone vibrates in my pocket. I ignore it, and we fall into a different conversation. But whoever it is is insistent.

"You'd better answer," Santiago says, hearing the buzzing.

I reach into my pocket and see it's Ezra, so I do because he'd leave a message unless it was urgent.

"Ezra?" Santiago drinks his scotch as he watches me.

"Judge. We've located the maid."

"Miriam?"

"Yes. She's in Florida. Enjoying the sun and sea."

"Give me an address."

"No need. I believe at this point it would be a waste of your time. I confirmed she was the one who gave Douglas your location the day of the attack on Mercedes. She also told him about her allergy." There's a pause, and I think I hear her in the background. "Tell me what you want me to do. I can go through legal channels." There's a silence. "Or not."

"Not," I tell him, angry but somehow calm. "A

limp, I think. Something that will remind her of what she did for the rest of her life."

"Understood," he says darkly. There's a moment of silence, then something clattering to the ground as a woman, Miriam, lets out an ear-piercing scream before I hear the clicking of a door and silence again. He is efficient and trustworthy, Ezra. Miriam will pay a dear price. "Oh," Ezra casually starts. "I spoke with Theron. He really is looking forward to a visit."

"I'll go at the end of the week," I assure him and disconnect the call to find Santiago's eyes still on me. He raises his eyebrows. "One down. One to go. Plus Hildebrand." I check the time and stand.

"You're sure you don't want me to go with you?" Santiago asks, standing too.

"No. Hildebrand has the idea I'll one day sit on The Tribunal. Let me use that. I'll let you know what I learn."

He extends his hand, and I take it. "Thank you, Judge. For everything you're doing for my family."

Guilt creeps in, but I nod because I don't trust myself to speak. And then I head toward the compound.

Predictably, Hildebrand is sitting in his office well into the evening. He is divorced, has no family in the New Orleans faction, and rarely visits his adult children or brothers on the East Coast.

Which is why he's so fucking committed to the letter of the law.

"Judge. I wasn't expecting you," he says as I'm shown into his office.

"I realize it's late, but I was passing by and thought I'd drop in. We have something to discuss, after all."

He looks at me like he doesn't quite follow, which is a ruse, but I play along.

"Ms. De La Rosa. I am her guardian, and as a law man myself, I will represent her if need be."

"Well, that is beneath your standing. You are a judge."

I shrug a shoulder. "I am not bothered by appearances or standing."

"What would Carlisle say about that, I wonder?" He and my grandfather were good friends. As far as men like that can be friends.

"I guess he'd turn over in his grave." I set my briefcase down and take a seat. "The Tribunal has called Ms. De La Rosa to appear based on the words of a convicted and executed killer."

"We'd like her to answer some questions. That's all. In fact, her staying away raises some eyebrows I can tell you."

"That hasn't been her choice. She is unaware of the summons. I've kept it from her."

"Why?"

I tilt my head, take a moment to study him,

then lean forward a little. "I'm going to be very honest with you. I feel she's more delicate than she lets on. And in my opinion, the matter being as inconsequential as I know it to be, it may behoove us all to allow me to mete out an appropriate punishment and move forward without dragging the De La Rosa name through the mud. It is after all a woman's game she played out of jealousy."

His eyebrows furrow. "A game?"

"The poisoning wasn't Mercedes's doing. We all know that. In hiring the courtesan, Mercedes simply wanted to make Ivy jealous. That's where her involvement ended."

"Ah." He leans back in his seat.

I do too. Crossing an ankle over my knee. But the sinking feeling in my gut grows the longer the silence drags on.

"Am I missing something, Councilor?"

"Well, yes, you are, Judge. And I'm not sure it's appropriate for you to be here."

"What is it that I am not aware of?"

"Nor is it appropriate for you to ask these questions outside of the space of The Tribunal." He stands.

I do too. But I don't leave. "Councilor, pardon my language, but what the hell is going on?"

He exhales, sets his jaw, and nods to the guard behind me to leave. And I know this is for show.

He will do me a favor now. One he'll hold over my head for years to come.

Once the guard is gone and the door closes, he opens a desk drawer and takes out a folder. He opens it. Inside are several printed pages of minutes. He turns it around so I can see it, and when I read the name of the interviewee, the ground drops out from beneath me.

Vincent Douglas.

"Lana Douglas's brother has been to see me. You know who she is. Or was, I should say."

I shift my gaze from the papers to his.

"Yes, I thought so. He asserts Lana was killed. Says he has evidence in the form of a surveillance video."

No. Santiago's men would not have missed that. "Surveillance?"

"Ms. Douglas never let go of the habit of making little videos it seems. Married men and the like. It's one of the reasons she was let go from the Cat House."

"So trustworthy was she. I'm sure her brother is the same. Where is this brother?"

"I've seen the footage, Judge. It's damning to Ms. De La Rosa." He doesn't mention Douglas's whereabouts, and I know it's on purpose.

"I'd like to see it for myself."

"It's locked in a safe. It will be presented once

she appears before The Tribunal, which she will voluntarily do within the week or else."

"Or else?"

He sighs. "Judge, this is very serious for her."

"I'd like to see the footage before I bring her to stand before The Tribunal. She is a De La Rosa. Remember that."

"We are all equals before The Tribunal."

I can hear the gossips already. If she's hauled in here, she'll be humiliated. And if the video surveillance truly shows what Hildebrand claims, it will be worse than humiliation. There will be payment. And it will be in the currency The Tribunal deals in and understands. Flesh.

He opens the same drawer to take out a flash drive.

"Because we are friends. Because of your standing and future here." He hands me the drive. I take it. "Your charge is in very serious trouble, Judge. I'll expect to hear from you tomorrow to arrange the time she will appear."

23

MERCEDES

"How are you feeling?" Solana's eyes move over me in appraisal as she takes a sip of her tea.

"Same as yesterday." I offer her an amused smile, but she doesn't return it. "And the day before that, and the one before that too."

I don't mention that Judge has been acting weird all week, leaving me vague instructions to get ready to go to the IVI compound this afternoon. Other than that, he's been keeping himself busy, and I have too.

"Mercedes, this is stressing me out." Solana sets her cup aside and glances at Georgie for backup. "You won't be able to hide this forever."

"I know." I shift on my seat, smoothing the hem of my dress over my legs. I'm already paranoid that someone will notice any day now that I'm dressing differently. That my stomach is softer and rounder.

"Do you really think Judge has no clue?" Georgie butts in.

"I'm pretty sure he thinks I'm just getting soft in the middle," I mumble. "I don't know. I'm not parading around naked in front of him in broad daylight, and I've avoided letting him near my belly. Let's just leave it at that."

"But you are still getting naked with him," Solana says. "He's going to notice any day now, whether it's in the dark or not."

I nod, accepting that they're right. I was slender to begin with, so that's worked to my advantage, but the clock is ticking, and I can't forget that.

"So?" Georgie looks at me expectantly.

"Soon," I choke out. "I'm figuring it out. My niece's baptism is in a couple of weeks. I don't want to do anything rash before then."

Solana doesn't look convinced, and Georgie is lost in his own thoughts. Neither one of them has any idea why I'm hesitating, but I can't stop thinking about my conversation with Judge. He opened up to me. He let me in, even if it was only for a little while. It feels like a slap in the face to leave him now, but what choice do I have? I know it doesn't change anything. He was giving me an explanation, not an opening to change his mind. If there's one thing I've figured out during my time with him, it's that Lawson Montgomery is not a man to be swayed once he's come to a decision. And I don't have the luxury of time to wait him out even if he was. I made this decision on my own, and I'll face the consequence on my own.

"Do you love him?"

Solana's innocent question sucks all the air from the room. I shake my head automatically in my default response. A De La Rosa doesn't show vulnerabilities like that. But even as I tell myself as much, it feels like a lie.

"That must be the reason," she says. "You're holding back. Are you sure there isn't something—"

The sound of the front door slamming interrupts her thoughts, and we all swivel our heads just in time to see Judge stalking into the sitting room. When he sees Solana and Georgie on the sofa, his eyes flare with irritation.

"Not today," he growls. "You two have to leave. Now."

"Judge." I glare at him as I rise to my feet, but he doesn't seem to hear me, or if he does, he doesn't show it.

"I need you both to leave right now," he clips out. "That's not a request. You can come back another day. Mercedes and I have somewhere to be."

"They aren't going anywh—"

My mouth snaps shut when his gaze moves to mine, and I know without a doubt I've never seen him like this. I can't tell what it is exactly, but something isn't right. I can feel it in the tension vibrating from him. The hard set of his jaw and the uncertainty in his eyes. He looks guarded, but there's something else too. Nervous, I think. And I have never once seen Judge nervous.

I swallow as he slices a finger in the direction of the door. "Mercedes, your brother will be here any minute. Get upstairs, now."

"Santi?" I choke out his name. "Is he okay?"

"Goddammit," Judge barks. "There's not time for questions. Please."

He drags a hand through his hair, and I nod, offering an apologetic glance at Solana and Georgie as they rise from their seats.

"It's okay," Solana says, but all the while, she's glaring at Judge. "We'll come back tomorrow. But text me tonight so I know you're okay."

Judge doesn't miss her inference, and Georgie shoots him a sharp look too. I feel like I should defuse this situation before things get any worse, but Judge doesn't give me a chance. He grabs me by the arm and hauls me from the room, calling out for Lois to escort my guests out. I give them one last fleeting glance before we turn the corner, and Judge is snapping at me again.

"I told you to be ready for this afternoon."

"I am." I try to yank my arm out of his grasp, but his hold is too tight. "Jesus, what's the big deal? I thought we were just going to a Society event. Why is Santi coming here?"

He doesn't answer me as he drags me into my old room and plunks me onto the chair. His eyes are wild as they move around the space as if he's only now realizing none of my stuff is in here.

"Stay put," he demands.

I frown at his retreating form and then promptly disobey him by scurrying over to the bed to hide the small burner phone Solana and Georgie brought me. There's enough time to stuff it under the pillow before I hear Judge's footsteps, and I dash back to the chair. He enters the room right as I'm recrossing my legs, eyes me suspiciously, and then starts to offload some of my things.

I stare at him like he's lost his mind as he tosses a few dresses onto the bed, a necklace onto the table, and one of my books onto the nightstand. And then it all falls into place. Is this why he's so out of sorts? Because he's terrified Santiago will realize Judge has been fucking me every night in his bedroom? The realization stings, but then, when doesn't it? Everything Judge dishes out comes with a side of pain.

"I suppose it wouldn't do to have him see I'm

sleeping in your bed every night?" I observe bitterly.

"No, it wouldn't fucking do," he clips out.

God, he really is in a mood today. And now I am too. So much so that even when Santi appears a moment later, hovering in the doorway, I can't seem to wipe the irritation from my face. He sees it, frowns, and then looks at Judge.

"Everything okay?"

"Yes," Judge grits out. "I'm just trying to get Mercedes ready."

I shoot him another withering glance at that lie, but he acts like he doesn't notice. Santi, however, definitely does, and the disappointment on his face is clear.

"Are you causing problems?"

"No." I cross my arms and stand. "I don't even know what the hell is going on. I thought we were just going to a Society event, and then Judge comes home all out of sorts—"

"You didn't tell her?" Santi arches a brow at Judge.

"No." Judge shifts, his discomfort obvious.

"Well, can somebody kindly tell me what the hell is going on?" I demand.

Santi sighs, scrubs a hand over his face, and I don't like the regret I see in his eyes when they fall back upon me. "You're being called before The Tribunal, Mercedes."

I don't know if it's the floor or my stomach that drops out as his words register. "What?"

"I thought we handled everything," he says quietly. "But it appears there's some evidence we didn't know about. It's been brought forward, and we have to go deal with this."

"Oh, my God." I nearly choke on the words, shaking my head as nausea unfurls in my gut.

"It's going to be okay," Judge tells me through clenched teeth, but even I can hear he doesn't know that for certain.

"What evidence?" I whisper. "What do they know?"

"You really should have told her." Santi frowns. "We don't have much time. We'll explain in the car. Is that what you're wearing?"

His eyes move over my flared baby doll dress, and I force a stiff nod. It's not my usual style at all, but it hides my curves, and he seems glad for it.

"That's good," Santi says approvingly. "You look... innocent."

His tone implies I'm far from it, but I don't have the energy to respond. I can barely think as they guide me out to the waiting car and help me inside. So many thoughts swirl around my mind that my head feels like it's going to explode.

I can't believe Judge didn't tell me about this. And on that note, why the hell didn't Santi? A deranged laugh almost bursts from my lips as I even consider it. Of course, they didn't tell me. Because this is how Society men are. They handle everything as they see fit. Everyone else be damned. If I actually expected anything else, I'm delusional.

I press my fingers to my temples and try to breathe as Santi explains how there's surveillance footage of me. How they know I was at the courtesan's apartment, and her brother has brought it forward to The Tribunal. He doesn't come out and say how bad this is, but he doesn't have to. I know. This isn't a matter of someone just disappearing. I'm linked directly to it, and that's a problem for The Society. Outside attention on these matters does not bode well for members. Everyone knows that. The consequences for something like this will be far worse than a slap on the wrist. They could toss me in a Tribunal prison cell. Or worse yet, they could actually demand physical punishment.

I'm starting to hyperventilate when I feel Judge's hand on my back, but it doesn't help. Nothing is going to make this better.

"Pull over!" I screech, slapping a hand against my mouth as I start to gag.

Past the blood pulsing through my ears, drowning out the noise, I vaguely hear some muttered curses. The car comes to a halt, and Judge doesn't even have time to help me out before

I'm crawling halfway over his lap and puking out the door.

"Oh, God," I choke out, another heave coming.

"It's okay." His hands hold me in place across his lap, my head hanging out over the ground as I puke again.

"Jesus," Santi mutters. "Mercedes, are you okay?"

I can't answer him because I'm too busy puking, but after a few minutes, it seems there's nothing left in my stomach. I'm weak and humiliated when Judge pulls me back into the middle seat, using a handkerchief to wipe my mouth.

"We need to postpone," he growls. "They'll have to accept that."

"They won't." Santi's tone makes me think this has already been postponed for some time.

They start to argue, so I intervene. "It's just the initial meeting, right?" I croak. "It will be okay. It's not the trial. Let's just get this part over with."

I can feel their gazes on me, but I don't dare look at them. I don't want them to see the fear in my eyes.

"It's just the initial meeting," Santi assures me. "You'll need to answer some questions today. That's it."

"Okay." I stare ahead at Raul. "Then let's go."

"Mercedes, so nice of you to finally join us," Hildebrand remarks dryly as he stares down at me from the dais in The Tribunal courtroom. Gone is his easy manner from the night we all had dinner together, and now I know I'm dealing with Councilor Hildebrand, rather than the man.

At his flank are two other councilors. They are the same men who presided over Abel's trial. The same men Ivy had to face when she was accused of poisoning my brother. I was here on both those occasions, and I know they are not men who will be swayed by the charms of any woman. They are all wearing severe expressions as they look down on me in shame, and if it weren't for Santi holding my arm, I might pass out entirely.

Judge is on my other side, his body rigid, and he's not touching me. I don't have to guess why. I'm certain he's already received a few strange looks from my brother as I was laid out across his lap hurling my lunch up.

"I'm waiting for a response, young lady," Hildebrand chides me, and Santi gives my arm a little squeeze as he speaks for me.

"It's my fault," he says, taking on the burden himself. "Mercedes wasn't aware of the situation at hand. We thought it best not to worry her. She's been... in a fragile state."

"Fragile, how?" Hildebrand arches a brow at me. "It didn't appear that way when she was at dinner, flirting away with Theron Montgomery without a care in the world."

I swallow when Santi clearly doesn't know how to respond to that, and I'm sure he'd like to believe I've lived without any guilt or remorse for the things I've done. But that's simply not true.

"If I may." Judge directs the councilor's attention to him, stepping forward in a way that shows no fear. And for a moment, it makes me feel like maybe things will be okay. Because he does this every day. He knows how these situations work. Only that's in the outside world. In our world, we all know nothing is ever certain.

"You may." Hildebrand nods at Judge.

"As you are aware, Mercedes has been in my care for quite some time."

"We are aware. A result of her involvement with her own brother's poisoning, no doubt."

Santi tenses beside me, and I want to look up at him and see his expression more than anything, but I know I can't.

"It was a result of many different factors," Judge replies coolly. "But first and foremost, I would say that it's a direct result of her grief, the loss of her family, and the uncertainty of navigating such dark times. I will be the first to admit that Mercedes has had her troubles, but I will also be the first to tell you that she has come leaps and bounds from the young woman I first took into my care. She has proven herself to be generous, intelligent, soft-hearted, and gracious. Mercedes De La Rosa is a Society daughter, and with that comes expectations. She has learned, as many of us have, to portray herself in a favorable light at all times, despite any turmoil that might be lingering beneath the surface. I can assure you that the Mercedes you saw at dinner is not an accurate representation of the many layers in her. She has put on a brave face for the world, but there is more... so much more to her than anyone could ever know. I'm kindly asking you to take this into consideration before we proceed with a messy trial that will tarnish her reputation or the De La Rosa name."

An uncomfortable silence falls over the courtroom as Judge's words settle over us all. I'm staring at the back of his head, my heart beating three times faster than I know it probably should. Santi's gaze is on him too. As are every pair of eyes up on the dais.

"I had no idea you had it in you to say so many thoughtful words about someone, Lawson," Hildebrand snorts. "But I suppose you've had your practice, haven't you? This is exactly the type of defense that would sway you in your own courtroom."

The councilor's response deflates me immediately, the small moment of comfort I felt from

Judge's testimony dissipating into the void. What Hildebrand said makes sense, and that's far easier to believe than the genuine sentiments from a man who's practically told me he's incapable of love.

"If you aren't here to listen to us testify to my sister's character," Santi interjects, "then what is the purpose of this charade?"

Hildebrand narrows his gaze at my brother before turning his appraising eyes on me. "Character testimony can be saved for later. You are correct in that, Santiago. Let's get on with the questions then, shall we?"

He gestures with his hand, and I see he has a remote. It's only after he presses a button that I realize they're actually going to show us the surveillance footage. I feel like I'm going to be sick all over again as the white screen at the front of the room flickers to life, and the video starts to play.

It's undoubtedly footage from Lana's apartment. I recognize the setting right away, my eyes moving to the very lamp I used to end her life. I clutch at my stomach, swaying slightly as Santi holds me tighter in his grasp. And then I watch in horror as one of the worst nights of my life is replayed for me.

On screen, I enter the apartment, pushing my way inside as soon as she opens the door. We have words. She laughs in my face, denies ever betraying me as she looks me in the eyes and tells me I'm insane. I grab her by the arm and tell her she's coming with me, trying to hold her hostage with the small knife in my other hand. In retrospect, it was a stupid move, but I wasn't thinking clearly. All I knew was that my brother had almost died again, and she had done it. She had poisoned him, and there was no alternative. She had to pay. But things didn't go the way I thought.

Lana had some kind of self-defense training, and it became obvious when she disarmed me quickly and tried to swing the knife at my throat. I blocked her with my purse and then threw it at her face before I launched myself at her with everything I had. We both tumbled to the floor, and the knife skittered beneath the sofa. But it didn't end there.

She came at me with an unexpected fury inside her, throwing her fists at my ribs, my chest, my throat, anywhere she could reach. I hadn't ever been in a physical fight before. I was fighting blindly, throwing out haphazard slaps and punches, when she flipped me onto my side and socked me in the gut so hard I couldn't breathe. Then she grabbed me by the hair, slamming my head against the floor, disorienting me. That's when she started to crawl for the knife, and I knew only one of us was getting out of there alive.

I don't even know how I staggered to my knees and grabbed the heavy glass lamp from the table.

It must have been a moment of adrenaline. A pure survival instinct. I didn't wait for her fingers to latch around the knife before I slammed the fat end of the lamp against the back of her skull. It made contact with a thud, and she grunted as she collapsed but recovered far too quickly. She was still reaching, still trying to get the knife, and I knew if she did, I was dead.

I don't know what came over me at that point, but it's obvious to everyone I was more animal than human as I hit her in the side of the face with all my might. All my rage boiled to the surface as she fell back and hit the floor with a sickening crack. But still she slapped weak hands at me, even as I crawled on top of her and thrust the lamp down in her face. Again and again and again, I released my pain and anger over what she'd done. At the life she almost stole from me. The only family I had left.

It wasn't until the glass finally shattered in my hands and my jarring bellows came to an abrupt halt that I realized she was no longer moving. Her face was unrecognizable. It was gory and disfigured, but it was the crimson oozing from her skull that sealed my fate. The reality I accepted far too slowly on the screen, holding my bloodied hands in front of me and releasing a heart-wrenching sob.

I watch silently as that alternate version of me

whispers in horror at the realization of what she's done. And even now, I can recall the pain lancing through my chest as I stupidly tried to revive her. As if I could. As if I wasn't a fucking monster.

"That's enough," Santi's choked voice echoes from beside me. "We get the point."

I can't bear to look at him. I know I can't. I'm too terrified of what I might see in his eyes.

"I think the film speaks for itself." Hildebrand uses the remote to turn off the screen, his eyes falling upon me again. "Will you deny what's obvious, Ms. De La Rosa? You were there. The proof is indisputable."

"I was there." I hang my head, trying to hold back my tears. "I won't deny it."

"It was self-defense," Santi snarls from beside me. "Anyone can see that."

Despite my assurance I wouldn't, I swivel my gaze to him, and more tears fill my eyes as I realize he's not just saying it. He really does believe that.

"It's quite obvious it became a battle to the death," Hildebrand concedes. "I will give you that. However, it doesn't negate the fact that she instigated the events by going there on her own in the first place. She hired the courtesan, and then when things went awry, she tried to cover up the incident. She acted in a manner completely at odds with what IVI represents. We do not allow these things to become outside issues. It's the one rule we must all abide by. Yet we now have an outsider insistent on retribution. Mercedes has drawn attention to us, and not in a good way. This must be dealt with, as much as it displeases me to say. There must be severe consequences—"

"Enough," Judge snaps. "I would like to have a word with you in private. Now."

Hildebrand narrows his gaze at Judge, and I cling to Santi as visions of public beatings taint my mind.

"We aren't finished," the councilor tells him.

"I'm invoking the Vicarius clause," Judge replies, low and quiet.

Hildebrand's eyes flare, and my brother tenses beside me, but I don't understand what that means. Before I have a chance to guess, Hildebrand shifts his attention to my brother.

"Remove her from his courtroom and wait outside. It looks like we'll be having that word in private after all."

24

JUDGE

I don't look at her. I can't. I don't trust myself. Instead, I keep my gaze on the councilors, hating Hildebrand as he watches Santiago remove Mercedes from the courtroom.

I know what is coming. What form the punishment will take. And I cannot and will not allow Mercedes to bear it. Not after the trauma she has already experienced at her father's hand and at Theron's. And even without those events, there was never a question that I would do this. That I would take her place.

Once the door closes behind them, Hildebrand turns his gaze to me, and I wonder if he's disappointed. Because the Vicarius clause will put her out of his reach.

And me squarely in it.

"I hope you know what you're doing, Judge," he says, adjusting his reading glasses and looking down at the folder before him.

I'm doing the only thing I can do.

I wonder how many members of The Society know of the Vicarius clause. Santiago does. I could feel him stiffen when I spoke the words to invoke it. Will he tell Mercedes its meaning? I doubt it. Because the matter at hand isn't the courtesan's death. That was self-defense. The surveillance leaves little to discuss on that. Our problem now is twofold. It's a matter of Mercedes lying, and perhaps more importantly, the fact that The Society is exposed to and made vulnerable to an outsider by her actions.

IVI may exist in its own bubble, but we are still a part of the outside world. We have to be. And I can imagine how news of a secret society would make headlines, outing members as both truth and fiction are fed to hungry consumers ready to cast stones.

The councilors converse quietly, Hildebrand with his hand over the microphone so I can't hear. Montrose, the eldest of the three and the one Hildebrand would have me replace, shakes his head. He is also the gentlest of the three. As far as they can be gentle. I think Hildebrand would have preferred Carlisle to sit in Montrose's seat, but as the terms of the councilors are lifetime, he could not be removed.

"Alright." Hildebrand removes his hand, drawing my attention as he clears his throat. "As a formality, I must ask you to state your understanding of the Vicarius clause, Mr. Montgomery." I am Mr. Montgomery in here. Not Judge Montgomery. As Hildebrand said a few nights ago, we are all equals before The Tribunal.

"In invoking the Vicarius clause, one makes the pledge to stand in the place of the party charged with wrongdoing and accepts the consequences on their behalf."

He nods.

"And you are willing to stand in the place of Mercedes De La Rosa and take her punishment?" Montrose asks.

I steel myself. "I am."

"How can you, not knowing what The Tribunal will demand? Isn't it foolhardy?" Hildebrand asks, and I know he is disappointed it's not Mercedes standing where I am now. I don't know if he has a fondness for punishing those of high rank or just women in general.

"That is not our concern, Councilor," Montrose says to him. "Once Vicarius is invoked, it cannot be undone. It is our law."

Yes, I know that too. But I wouldn't undo it. I

will not allow them to lay a hand on her even at the cost of my own flesh.

"Yes, you are right, Councilor," Hildebrand acknowledges, then turns back to me. "We all know the facts, agreed, Mr. Montgomery?"

"Agreed."

"The charges are serious, and in invoking Vicarius, you save this court the trouble of a hearing. You admit guilt and submit yourself to the penalty."

"Correct."

"Due to Mercedes's actions, she has opened The Society up to the scrutiny of the outside world. This brother of the courtesan..." He looks down at the papers before him. "Vincent Douglas. He will not simply go away. He wished to witness Ms. De La Rosa's sentence carried out, but we would not allow that. We punish our own, but we also protect our own. The Tribunal will absorb the cost of his silence."

"Very generous," I say.

"It is." He closes the folder and sighs deeply. "As we discussed previously, each member of The Society is equal before The Tribunal. And as such, the sentence passed down to you would be the same as if it were any other member."

I nod, wishing he'd get on with it. I have an idea what to expect. But I won't know the extent of it until he spits it out and I think he enjoys this too much to rush.

"For her offenses in the law we are all guided by, which we must follow to the letter, Ms. De La Rosa is hereby sentenced to the maximum penalty."

My heart slows to a heavy thud against my chest.

"Which in a case with such grave consequences to The Society as a whole is twenty-four lashes."

I don't move. Don't breathe. Don't blink. All while blood rushes my brain.

Twenty-four lashes. Christ. Mercedes would not be able to withstand that, and they would revive her every time she passed out before continuing. She would be made to feel every single one of those twenty-four strokes.

"Given the delicate state of this matter, it would behoove The Tribunal to keep this proceeding a secret and not upset the general population. No public announcement will be made. And the lashes will be dealt in private."

Well, there is that. "I understand."

"All that remains is a date to be set—"

"Now," I say, speaking before I can think.

Hildebrand appears surprised. "That is out of the ordinary. I will choose a—"

"It is my right, Councilor." I know IVI law to the letter as well as he does.

"Yes, Judge, it is. So be it." He closes the folder, and the gavel comes down at the same time as he gestures to one of the guards standing by to escort me. I am then led through the door to a passage that will carry us to the cells and, at their center, the interior space where punishment in these delicate matters, as Hildebrand put it, are meted out.

I don't think. I walk. And no one lays a hand on me as we enter the large space, one I've seen multiple times. One where I've borne witness.

There, I take off my jacket and vest. I tuck my cuff links into my pocket and remove my shirt. Mercedes would be made to strip naked. It's how the women are handled. Not the men, though. I hear some of the things she's said to me over the past few months, about how women are treated as second-class citizens within The Society. And she's right. We are not all equal before The Tribunal. Not even close.

A guard steps forward to bind my wrists to the poles, but I shake my head. "Not necessary."

"It is customary."

"No."

He hesitates but nods and steps back. He will witness and report back to the councilors that the tithe was paid. And once it's over, Mercedes will be free. They will not be able to punish her for this.

It's that thought that gives me the courage to step between the ancient wooden beams worn by centuries of use. It's her face I see as I wrap the chains around my hands where I would have been secured and hold tight. And it's her eyes I envision looking up at me in that way she has when she's lying in my arms as I nod, and it begins.

25

MERCEDES

"Santi, what does that mean?" I wring my hands together in my lap as we sit outside the courtroom, waiting in stilted silence.

My brother's been staring at the wall for the last ten minutes, and I can't get a read on him.

"I don't know just yet," he answers quietly.

I don't believe for one second that's true, but I also know there's no point in pushing him when he's like this. He seems lost in his own thoughts, and I'm not expecting him to say anything else. So when he turns to me with anguish in his eyes, it unsettles me deeply.

"I've been unfair to you," he rasps. "I didn't... I didn't realize."

"What?" I blink up at him, my eyes burning

with more emotion I want to blame on the hormones but can't.

"I was so angry with you." He shakes his head, disgusted by the admission. "I shouldn't have been so cruel that night."

I turn my gaze to the floor, understanding this is his guilt. He saw the video, and it clearly rattled apart the image he had concocted in his own mind. Though, I'm not certain what kind of person he must have believed me to be if he truly thought I went to Lana's apartment to murder her in cold blood.

"I knew it never fit," he goes on. "But I had to hold on to my anger. After everything you'd done—"

"I know." I close my eyes and swipe at the tears that fall. "I'm sorry, Santi."

He reaches toward me, his hand pausing before he touches my shoulder hesitantly. When I meet his gaze, I can see that he's still the same old Santi in many ways. He's awkward with affection and comfort, but it's obvious his wife has softened him in that aspect too.

"We will put this behind us soon," he promises me. "And you'll be a part of our lives again. We'll figure out a way to—"

The door to the courtroom opens, and a guard appears, his gaze moving right past me to my brother. "The councilors direct you to take Ms. De La Rosa home. This meeting will continue, and Mr. Montgomery will rejoin you later."

I stare past him through the crack, but I can't hear anything, and I don't understand. What could Judge possibly be doing in there? The thought unnerves me, but Santiago seems relieved by the development.

"Thank you." He rises, and the guard disappears back into the courtroom, sealing us outside.

I'm staring at the door when Santi helps me up, but I don't want to leave. Because I know what this development means, even if I don't know what's happening beyond that door. I've known it since they hauled me into the car and delivered me here, and I don't want to leave without one last look at Judge. One last goodbye.

"Mercedes." Santi's voice snaps me from my thoughts, and I look at him in a daze. "We have to go."

I force a nod, dragging my feet as I follow him out to the car. The entire way, I'm considering if I could wait. If there's still time to have one more night with Judge when he returns. But in my heart, I know there's not. There can't be. He'll be even more alert with this hanging over my head. He'll probably suspect I'd want to run because he thinks I'm a coward. But the truth is, I don't have a choice.

If I want to spare the child growing inside me from whatever archaic punishment they might see fit to dole out, I have to do this today.

Judge won't understand it. Neither will Santiago. And those thoughts turn my stomach the entire drive back to the Montgomery estate. I only just got my brother back. But I know when I glance at him, this is the lesser evil. He will be disappointed in me for running but not nearly as disappointed in me as he would be if he knew the truth. If he knew I was ruined for any eligible man, that I'd thrown away my virtue and left yet another stain on our family name, all that would be left is shame.

I can't bear that. I can't allow my child to suffer shame for existing. And I won't allow my baby to come to harm at the hands of The Tribunal. No matter what I do now, there will be damning consequences. I will never be looked upon favorably. If I told them I was pregnant, they might spare me a beating until the baby is born, but there's no guarantee. IVI is an institution heavily influenced by Catholicism, but as a Society daughter, I think I've been shielded in many ways from some of the gory details about the punishments they mete out in circumstances like mine. I just watched them execute Abel Moreno, and while rare, these things do happen. There's too much uncertainty about what they might want to do with my child, especially once they learn the father never wanted it to begin with. My future here is too unpredictable, and I have no choice. I know it in my gut, even as my heart wrenches at the thought.

The car pulls to a stop far too soon, and I blink, startled by the realization that I'm home already. *Home.* The word seems strange as I stare out the window in a daze, but that's exactly what Judge's house feels like. Only it can never truly be my home.

"Mercedes." Santi's voice infiltrates my thoughts. "Judge hasn't been inappropriate with you, has he?"

His words linger between us, and for one delusional moment, I consider what would happen if I just told him the truth. If I asked for my inheritance and to be free of the chains surrounding me. Would he let me go?

I glance at his reflection in the window, and I know I'm clinging to a false hope. So I do what I've always done. I choke down the sadness in my throat and force a laugh.

"Come on, Santi. Get real. We both know Lawson Montgomery has no intentions of falling in love."

When I walk into the house, it's quiet, and I know that means Lois is either out with the dogs or at her cottage. The antique clock in the entryway tells me it's almost four o'clock, and I don't know how long Judge will be gone, but I know this will probably be the only opportunity I have.

It isn't until I'm in my old room, grabbing the burner phone from beneath the pillow that a realization occurs to me. It's Friday.

"Oh, my God." I dart from my room and run down the hall as quietly as I can manage, fumbling with the screen on the phone as I check the time.

I have ten minutes, if my calculations are correct. It almost seems too good to be true. Like fate or kismet has intervened to give me this opportunity on exactly this day. Because every Friday without fail, I know Paolo goes to town to pick up supplies for the horses and dogs.

I don't really have a plan as I skid into the foyer and clutch the phone in my palm, but I know I'll have to figure something out. There are still guards out front, and there's a good chance they could stop me from heading for the stables. But Judge has been letting me go as long as Paolo is around. Will they check Paolo's truck if they don't know where I am?

As I'm considering it, I come to an abrupt halt right before I open the door. *Shit.* My necklace. It's the one thing I wanted to take with me. The one thing I have from Judge. Indecision paralyzes me as I glance between the stairs and the clock. I don't want to leave it behind. But I've already wasted three minutes, and my heart is beating so hard that I think I will miss this chance if I go back.

"I can't." I squeeze my eyes shut and shake my head, trying to put it from my mind. "I can't."

I release a shaky breath and open the door, wrenching myself out of it. All three guards turn to look at me as I do, and I force a smile. There's no point in not letting them see me. If I went through the side door, they'd be far more suspicious.

"What are you doing?" the guy in charge asks.

"I'm going to brush the horses," I tell them without waiting for an answer.

Part of me is half expecting them to stop me, but as I walk on wooden legs, I hear them mutter something before returning to their conversation, something about another guard getting his mistress knocked up.

I suck in a breath and try to quicken my pace without being obvious, slipping into the stables and darting through to the other side. They can't see the back side of the building, and I'm just praying Paolo isn't already at his truck. I ease open the rear stable door as quietly as I can manage, and I hear Paolo whistling somewhere nearby. It makes me pause, but I can't tell what direction it's coming from.

Regardless, I decide I don't have a choice. I'm going to risk it. I step out and shut the door behind me, eyeing Paolo's truck a good twenty feet away. I don't know if he'll see me running to it, but when I hear him jangling his keys, I figure it's now or never.

I dart from the stables to the truck as quietly as my legs can carry me. Luckily, I'm light on my feet, and Paolo doesn't stop whistling, a good indication he's in his own little world. Even so, I'm still convinced he's going to figure it out as I fling myself up onto the bumper and into the truck bed. It creaks as I lower myself onto my hands and knees, and I curse when I hear Paolo's whistling falter. There's a long moment of silence, and then he grumbles something to himself. I peek through the back window to see he's dropped his keys on the way over here, and I release a silent prayer as I quietly edge myself as far beneath the toolbox as I can manage. When I've done that, I wait, hoping against hope he doesn't check the truck bed before he gets inside.

One minute passes. Then two. And then finally, I hear the telltale sound of him opening the door and climbing into the cab, and I breathe a sigh of relief. He fires up the engine, and the truck bed rattles against me as we roll forward over the unpaved earth.

I still feel like I can't breathe as I count the seconds and wait for the guards to inevitably stop us. I'm so certain it's going to happen that I have to suppress the urge to puke all over again. Every time I've tried to escape this place, something has dragged me back, and I'm convinced this time will be no different. But as I'm holding my breath, counting the tops of the trees that line the drive, the truck slows and then comes to a halt at what I know must be the gate. And I think this is it. I know there's a guard out here too. He's going to look. He's going to capture me.

Instead, the gate whirs open, the truck rolls forward, and I realize with equal parts terror and relief that that didn't happen. Paolo pulls onto the main roadway, and I fight the tears stinging my eyes as I wish for one last look at Judge's estate.

My home.

That word reverberates through my skull until I pull myself together and open my phone. I shoot a text to Solana with trembling fingers, letting her know I've made it out. She's already texted me a bunch of times, and I can see she's been worried based on what she saw this afternoon.

Immediately, my phone vibrates with another flood of texts as I consider my next steps. I answer her in a daze, thinking through my plans. My condo will be the first place Judge looks for me, and I'm sure the guards will alert him soon enough when they figure out their mistake. But I have to go there to get the cash I've hidden, which is my only resource at this point. After that, I don't know what. I just know I'll have to leave this city. I'll have to go far, far away and even then, they'll probably never stop looking for me.

As I consider everything and everyone I'll have to leave behind, an ache unlike any I've ever known spreads through my chest, icing my veins and freezing my heart. Solana's name flashes across my screen again, but there isn't time to read her message because Paolo's truck comes to a stop, and he turns it off. I wait for a full minute, completely still as he gets out, slams the door, and walks away.

From the sound around us, I can tell we're at the store. But I'm still not convinced if I pop up, there won't be guards everywhere, ready to drag me back. Back to The Tribunal. Back to the consequences of my actions from a time I couldn't know what I'd have to protect.

It's that thought that drives me to move. To jump out of the truck and run. I run until my lungs burn and my muscles seize from the exertion. It takes me a few minutes to find my bearings, but once I'm on a main thoroughfare, I flag down a taxi and jump inside, rattling off the address to my condo.

The cabbie drives me in silence. All the while, my phone continues to vibrate in my lap, but I can't look at it. I can't do anything but drag in each breath and focus on the next. I do that until we get to the place I once thought of as my sanctuary. Now it feels like anything but.

"Can you wait here?" I pay the cabbie when he pulls to a stop. "I'll just be a few minutes."

"No can do," he grumbles. "This was my last fare."

I release a frustrated sigh when I check my pockets, but I only have a few more dollars on me. It's not enough to tempt him to stay, and I'll just have to figure something else out when I leave. With a muttered thanks, I slam the door behind me and run to my condo, snatching the spare key from beneath the potted plant. I'm acting on muscle memory as I unlock the door and dart inside without a second thought, only to come to a dead stop when my sandals crunch over broken glass. That's when I realize with painstaking slowness that my condo has been trashed.

"What the—?" My words falter when a masked man steps out from the shadows and stalks toward me.

My first instinct is to scream, and as I pivot, he snatches me by the fabric of my dress, yanking me back against his body. He's large and strong, and a combination of terror and weakness is making me too slow to react. To think. But still, I try to fight him as he hauls me toward the back door. I slam my foot down on his, and he grunts, his grip on me tightening as he whispers one sentence with such finality it sends a shiver down my spine.

"Stop fighting before you really get hurt."

26

JUDGE

When I am released many hours later, Santiago is waiting by his car. I walk on wooden legs to meet him, each slow step an agony.

Pain. It's all I can think right now. Pain.

And her.

Dawn is breaking, but it's still dark enough that the streetlamp casts an eerie shadow over his tattooed face. He leans against the Rolls Royce, hands in his pockets, face set in stone. I wonder how long he's been here. A while, I think.

Without a word, he opens the door, and I sit, wincing as my back brushes against the leather of the seat. He looks at me, but swallows back his comment. In silence, we drive to De La Rosa Manor.

The house is quiet. Everyone is still sleeping,

I'm sure. We walk to his office, and when I enter, Ivy stands up from where she was lying on the sofa. She must have fallen asleep here. For the first time in all the time I've known her, she doesn't look at me with fear but something else.

"Sit," Santiago says, taking my briefcase from me. I hadn't realized I was still holding it.

I sit and happily take the generous tumbler of scotch, trying not to wince as the movement of my arm disturbs the opened skin of my back. We both drink, and he refills our glasses.

"Is Mercedes alright?" I ask, my voice sounding close to normal. I think.

"She is."

"Good."

"Why did you do it?"

I don't tell him I couldn't ever let them hurt her for reasons I myself am only just beginning to understand.

"I knew the punishment, and I couldn't let her take it. I'm not sure it wouldn't break her entirely. And frankly speaking, if I hadn't invoked Vicarius, wouldn't you have?"

He drops his gaze to the floor and nods. "What was it?"

"Twenty-four lashes."

Ivy gasps from her place across the room, and I turn to her and raise an eyebrow. I give her a smile. "I survived."

"Santiago, the painkillers. They'll help," Ivy says as if just remembering.

"No, no pills," I say. "Scotch will do it."

"Are you sure?" she asks.

I nod. Santiago is watching me when I turn back to him, and I swallow the second scotch, then hold my glass out for another. He fills it generously.

"Besides, Hildebrand would have enjoyed punishing Mercedes too much," I say. "I have a feeling he'd have happily stood witness."

"I am sure he enjoyed punishing you, too. He's a fucking sadist. Take off your shirt and let's see the mess they've made."

I stand and am slow to peel it off, hissing with pain as the skin reopens when I pull the shirt away. Their doctor cleaned the wounds, and that may have been more painful than the actual lashing, but when Santiago walks behind me, and I hear his intake of breath, I have a feeling I'll be going through it again.

"Fucking barbarians. Sit down, Judge. And help yourself to the scotch. Ivy, come help me. Your touch is gentler than mine."

I look over my shoulder to see her take in the damage, her eyes growing misty, mouth frozen in an O. But then I see Santiago's face. His gaze on the tattoo he doesn't know about. At least I hope the scar it covers is camouflaged by all the rest of the damage.

He clears his throat and meets my eyes. He won't be asking me about that tonight.

Turning the chair, I straddle it, and for the next half hour, I endure another round of cleaning and bandaging. I drink half the bottle of scotch as they tend to the wounds.

"You were brave," Ivy says.

I am not sure about that. Maybe it was me atoning for my own sins against my friend whose keen eyes study me as he wipes his hands on a towel. Because I have broken his trust. I have bedded his sister again and again and again.

"I'll leave you two," Ivy says. She kisses her husband and leaves the room.

Santiago opens the armoire, and from a drawer, he tosses me one of his shirts. "Put this on. Yours is ruined." My bloodstained shirt lies on the floor. I pick it up and drop it in the trash can then put on his shirt. We're about the same size.

"How much did you tell Mercedes?" I ask him.

"Nothing. She doesn't know what the Vicarius clause is."

"Good."

"She should know what you did for her."

"I think she's learned her lesson, don't you? No need to burden her with more guilt."

He watches me still, and I wonder if it's my

guilt he sees. "We talked, my sister and me. And we will heal. I know that for sure now."

"I'm glad." But does this mean he'll take her back now? Take her from me? "If you'll lend me a car, I'd like to get home. I'll have Raul bring it back tomorrow."

"Why don't you stay? Get some sleep."

I shake my head. "I'd like to get home." *To her.*

"I'll drive you."

27

JUDGE

The dense oaks filter sunlight along the drive toward the Montgomery house. I watch the mammoth building come into view and am reminded of the night I brought Mercedes here so many months ago. So much has happened since then. So much has changed.

"Alright?" Santiago asks as he pulls to a stop before the front entrance.

I blink and turn to my friend. Would he be that if he knew what I've done? Would he forgive me? I try for a smile, my betrayal a stone in my gut.

"Thank you," I say.

"I believe it is us who owe you the thanks." He touches my shoulder lightly, but I still feel it as if he were gripping hard. I think this is the extent of Santiago showing his emotions. And he's come a long way. "Get some sleep."

"You too." I open the door and climb the stairs to the front entrance as Santiago drives away. But before I even reach it, Paolo pulls it open, and Lois comes running out after him, their faces dark with fatigue and worry.

My heart instantly drops to my stomach.

"We've been trying to call you. Where have you been?" Lois asks, too emotional to say more. Paolo lays a hand on her arm, and she quiets.

"What is it?" I ask, instinctively looking up to my bedroom window, realizing my phone is still switched off and in my briefcase.

Paolo takes a breath in, then turns to Lois. "Go inside. Make coffee."

She nods, wringing her hands, but seems grateful to be away and have something to do.

"What the fuck is going on?"

"Mercedes is gone."

"Gone? What? How?"

"She told the guards she was going to brush the horses yesterday around four in the afternoon. No one's seen her since. And I know for a fact she wasn't brushing the horses. When she didn't come down for dinner, Lois went upstairs to check on her and found both bedrooms empty."

"What? She can't have gone anywhere between the gates and the guards..."

"We've had men search the grounds, every cottage, for hours, Judge." He drops his head guiltily. "The timing... I took the truck like I always do to get the supplies for the horses. It's the only way I can think of that she'd have gotten off the property without being seen. I never checked the truck bed. I never do."

"She's gone?"

He nods. "I'm so sorry, Judge."

"You're sure you've searched everywhere?"

"I'm telling you she's not here."

Raul rushes out the front door, pulling his jacket on. He must have just gotten in. Where would she go? Solana? Georgie?

I dig my phone out of the briefcase and hand the case to Paolo. While it slowly comes back to life, I tell Paolo to let me know if anything changes at the house.

"Raul, get the car." I dial Ezra. It's early, but he answers, and I know I've woken him from the groggy sound of his voice. "Ezra."

There's a pause. He must hear the urgency in my tone. "What's happened, Judge?"

"I need the contacts of the men stationed at Georgie's and Solana's houses."

"I'll send them to you now."

"Thank you." I disconnect as Raul pulls up and move as quickly as I am able into the car. "Head into town," I tell him and dial the guards one at a time, but they both tell me Georgie and Solana's houses are quiet and have been all night.

"Her condo," I tell Raul and instruct the men to let me know as soon as they see Solana or Georgie. All the while, I'm trying to keep my mind from wandering to Vincent Douglas. To how he wanted to witness Mercedes's punishment but was told he could not. I doubt he'd believe she would be punished, considering. And then he'd set off on his own to avenge his sister's death once again.

Why would she run? Fear of what The Tribunal would do to her? I'd protect her. Doesn't she know that? I wouldn't let them touch her.

But it doesn't matter. I need to find her before Douglas does. She ran, and she's on her own. She'll need money which she had a lot of stashed at the condo. It's not there anymore, but she doesn't know that, so that's where she'd go. I'm sure of it.

Traffic slows us down as we get into town, and when we're a few blocks from the condo, I get out to walk, instructing Raul to meet me there. It'll be faster. I hurry through the streets, imagining what I must look like when people clear out of my way. I haven't slept. I've been beaten. And although adrenaline has burned the alcohol out of my system, I'm sure I'm a sight.

But I don't care. Because I need to get to her. Bring her home.

Does Douglas know about the condo? Because he's more dangerous than ever now. That's where my mind goes as I get to the small complex with its white picket fences and families ushering children into minivans to be driven to school. I don't miss their looks as I push open the gate of Mercedes's condo and am slightly relieved when I see a light on upstairs.

I have my own key. I had one made, but that, along with the rest of my keys, is in my briefcase. I lift the pot to use the spare she keeps but find the space empty. The key is gone. It's Mercedes. It has to be. She'd need to use it to enter.

I hear the Rolls screech to a stop once Raul arrives. I try the doorknob expecting to find it locked, but it's not. I push it open, calling out her name as I charge into the house and immediately stop.

Because the living room and kitchen are destroyed. Furniture overturned, glasses and dishes shattered.

Raul walks inside and mutters a curse.

"Upstairs," I tell him, and he takes the stairs two at a time.

A breeze blows in from the partially open patio door, and I take a step then another, then call out her name but get no answer.

"Nothing. There's no one here."

I walk through the living room, my mind not quite processing. Not wanting to. And there, just outside the patio door, I see her shoe. Just the one.

I recognize it from the pair she wore when we went to The Tribunal. It's beside an overturned pot, the plant that was inside it spilling out.

And caught on a splintered post of the little gate that leads down to the grassy path into the woods is a ripped scrap of her dress blowing in the early morning breeze. I pick up the shoe, my heart thudding against my chest as the gate loudly swings closed, then open again, and I rush down the stairs calling out her name, hurrying into the woods beyond.

Although I know she's not here. She's gone. Long gone. And so is whoever took her.

THANK YOU

Thanks for reading *Her Rebellion*. We hope you love Mercedes and Judge.

Their story concludes in Their Reign available in all stores.

ALSO BY A. ZAVARELLI

Kingdom Fall

A Sovereign Sons Novel

The Society Trilogy

Requiem of the Soul

Reparation of Sin

Resurrection of the Heart

Ties that Bind Duet

Mine

His

Boston Underworld Series

Crow

Reaper

Ghost

Saint

Thief

Conor

Sin City Salvation Series

Confess

Convict

Bleeding Hearts Series

Echo

Stutter

Standalones

Stealing Cinderella

Beast

Pretty When She Cries

Tap Left

Hate Crush

For a complete list of books and audios, visit http://www.azavarelli.com/books

ALSO BY NATASHA KNIGHT

The Rite Trilogy

His Rule

Her Rebellion

Their Reign

The Devil's Pawn Duet

Devil's Pawn

Devil's Redemption

To Have and To Hold

With This Ring

I Thee Take

Stolen: Dante's Vow

The Society Trilogy

Requiem of the Soul

Reparation of Sin

Resurrection of the Heart

Dark Legacy Trilogy

Taken (Dark Legacy, Book 1)

Torn (Dark Legacy, Book 2)

Twisted (Dark Legacy, Book 3)

Unholy Union Duet

Unholy Union

Unholy Intent

Collateral Damage Duet

Collateral: an Arranged Marriage Mafia Romance

Damage: an Arranged Marriage Mafia Romance

Ties that Bind Duet

Mine

His

MacLeod Brothers

Devil's Bargain

Benedetti Mafia World

Salvatore: a Dark Mafia Romance

Dominic: a Dark Mafia Romance

Sergio: a Dark Mafia Romance

The Benedetti Brothers Box Set (Contains Salvatore, Dominic and Sergio)

Killian: a Dark Mafia Romance

Giovanni: a Dark Mafia Romance

The Amado Brothers

Dishonorable

Disgraced

Unhinged

Standalone Dark Romance

Descent

Deviant

Beautiful Liar

Retribution

Theirs To Take

Captive, Mine

Alpha

Given to the Savage

Taken by the Beast

Claimed by the Beast

Captive's Desire

Protective Custody

Amy's Strict Doctor

Taming Emma

Taming Megan

Taming Naia

Reclaiming Sophie

The Firefighter's Girl

Dangerous Defiance

Her Rogue Knight

Taught To Kneel

Tamed: the Roark Brothers Trilogy

ABOUT NATASHA KNIGHT

Natasha Knight is the *USA Today* Bestselling author of Romantic Suspense and Dark Romance Novels. She has sold over a million books and is translated into six languages. She currently lives in The Netherlands with her husband and two daughters and when she's not writing, she's walking in the woods listening to a book, sitting in a corner reading or off exploring the world as often as she can get away.

Write Natasha here: natasha@natasha-knight.com

NATASHA KNIGHT

www.natasha-knight.com

ABOUT A. ZAVARELLI

A. Zavarelli is a USA Today and Amazon bestselling author of dark and contemporary romance.

When she's not putting her characters through hell, she can usually be found watching bizarre and twisted documentaries in the name of research.

She currently lives in the Northwest with her lumberjack and an entire brood of fur babies.

Want to stay up to date on Ashleigh and Natasha's releases? Sign up for our newsletters here: https://landing.mailerlite.com/webforms/landing/x3s0k6